TRUST

IN THE LORD

AND

OBEY

THE LAWS OF THE STREET

BOOK 1

WRITTEN BY
KELLI BROOKS

II

Dedicated to my Creative Dad, Duane Archer (my Mentor)

PRESENT DAY: UNITY POLICE STATION 2004

My daddy the now late, Pastor Braxton C. Simms of Mt. Emerald Baptist Church in Unity FL. Often told me, trust in the lord Babygirl, but always obey the laws of the streets."

His words are replaying in my head as I open the door of the police station and walk up to the front desk, Mrs. Suthers looks up at me, Child, aren't you supposed to be watching that handsome husband of yours being ordained as the new pastor of your father's church?" I look down at my all black, off the shoulder, and covered in rose gold sequins ball gown that I had custom made for this special night. My husband raved when I came downstairs in it earlier this evening, making it clear with his words and eyes that he cannot wait to get me back home.

"Yes ma'am, I'm just coming from the church." "Is the Chief in Mrs. Suthers?" "No, honey, he should be back soon maybe I can help you." concern starts to appear on her face. "I don't think that you can, is there a deputy around by any chance." I ask. "Girl, why are you here?"

It's not that I don't remember the reason I am here. I just know when I say it that means I really did it. "I shot that handsome husband of mine, about 15 minutes ago, I figure it's best if I should just come and turn myself in." I let out a deep sigh relieved to finally get that off my chest.

"Go sit in that chair over there," she orders. The sweet southern cadence gone from her voice. I make my way over to the chair she is pointing at however I sit in the chair next to it, to be petty. I've never been good with people telling me what to do, especially if they aren't asking in a polite manner. I keep in mind that I did just tell her that I shot my husband.

The burdens and confusion that have been on my heart and in my mind for the last 5 months, since my daddy had been murdered in front of my husband and I, are now gone. I put my trust in the Lord to guide me and let me see better than I hear. Things were starting to get foggy, but who I would have to take down to get the only justice I believe in is unthinkable and hasn't processed within me yet.

Unfortunately, everything led back to the love of my life, also the ones I consider family. I know that love is a lot of things, the Bible is clear on that, so I know what love is not. Husband or not I had to obey the laws of the streets.

I figure I'll be here for a while; I'm trying to get as comfortable as possible in this small chair. Looking up at the ceiling trying to focus on a pattern. All that is coming to my mind is… How in the fuck did I get here?

CHAPTER I

I wanted my dad to say, 'no' about going to this 'study session' with my best friend Simone, however he believes it would be a good idea. My dad thinks that I need a more active social life, I even told him that boys are going be there and he still did not care, "I know that you are a pastor's daughter, but I will not keep you from experiencing the world".

It's not like I'm not social I'm a cheerleader, the thing is I don't care for the high school politics, popularity stuff. My best friend on the other hand is complete opposite of me. She's been popular since elementary school. Simone is an only child like me, her mom is more interested in being her friend than being her mom. For the most part Simone raises herself. She lacks a father figure. I get it, because I lack a mother figure, other than the women at church that 'private sessions' with my dad. Those women try hard with him to win the spot of being 'First Lady' as well as the stepmom they feel I need in my life, or the women at the church say I act out because of the lack of female presence in our household. My dad is the definition of a 'playa pastor', slick with his words making it easy to keep his congregation, especially the women coming back, and staying devoted.

Simone and I are in our sophomore year at Unity High, she is ahead of me on the social scale, (in many ways). She's been hanging with the high school crowd since were in middle school. All I know is opposites do attract, we share two things in common our love for each other, also we have quick tempers, meaning we will pop a bitch fast, disrespect towards either of us is a no go. My dad taught me early, to argue is to waste energy, he doesn't promote violence, however he is not against it.

I'm trying to keep a straight face right now and not laugh. Simone is walking in front of me full speed ahead, she is in a hurry to get to her boyfriend Quan, I not trying to figure out what this argument is going to be about. Whatever it's about I know that it is serious. I can vaguely hear her talking to herself, maybe she's trying to calm herself down, or she is rehearsing how and what she plans on saying.

****

Here's the thing, when we were in the 8th grade Simone went to a kickback, (I'm not sure which one) and in her words, when telling me about that night, "he just had to have her". She decided to give in, it's not like she was a virgin. They both enjoyed what took place between them. So, after that night they began hooking up on the regular.

Quan was a sophomore at the time and claimed that he had never encountered Simone before that night. Which would have been believable, because the middle and high school are not on the same street. Majority of the blacks in Unity live on the 'block', one big circle divided into four streets. Quan and Simone live on the same street, on the same side of the sidewalk, and 3 houses down from each other. Simone walks pass his house going and coming from school, that's just the minimum, because she is always on the go.

One beautiful day, (kidding! But the day was beautiful) Simone called me crying like a baby, I didn't let her get out too many words, before I was headed out of my house. I got to her house in 3 minutes, record timing. When I got up to her room, she quickly gets to the reason for the crying. "Quan broke up with me, talking about I lied to him about my age." She began to cry in a more hysterical way after telling me that information. I looked around at all the pink Simone's room is decorated in, I hate pink, black is my favorite color. I walked over to her window, I wasn't angry at the breakup, or the stupid excuse Quan chose to use to end things. My anger was coming from the tears falling from my best friend's face.

While looking out of Simone's window, glad she didn't have her blinds down, I saw Quan pulling into the driveway of his house. "My nigga," I whispered under my breath. I grabbed Simone by the hand and rushed out of her house. I didn't say anything, because I knew that she would have backed out of what I felt necessary to do at the time.

"Quan!", I yelled as he was about to open the front door of the house. This dude turned around, and peeped the scene looking in every direction, he looked everywhere, but didn't look at Simone, standing behind me crying. He walked down the steps of the front porch and stood in front of us, well over us there's was a huge height difference.

My Grandma Eve says, "the bigger they are the harder they fall, remember what happened to Goliath". I was determined to test that theory.

He looked down at me locking eyes. "What's up shortie?" he asked me, still ignoring that there is a girl standing behind me that he has been having sex with. I could hear her sniffling. His dick must be amazing to cause all those tears. I should have slapped him for asking such a stupid question. "Quick question, why is my best friend crying?" I raised my eyebrows. "Come on, she tried to play me, lying about her age, and Quan doesn't mess with babies." He answers with a straight face still holding eye contact with me. I was finally close enough to Quan to get a good look at Simone's dude, I can't deny that his swag was captivating, and I knew then if he continued to take care of himself, he will only keep evolving into a dangerously handsome black man. However, I needed to stay focused.

Quan's mom is a devoted member to our church, he attends every blue moon. I sit in the balcony for privacy reasons. So, I've only seen him from afar, that day was the first day that I've seen him up close or spoken a word to him. His cologne was starting to distract me. I decided to focus in on the way he referred to himself in the third person, which caused me to assume he three things: runs off his ego, he is lacking in intelligence, or he may have different personalities.

"Nigga, save that shit for the hoes without a brain, you knew Simone wasn't in high school the first time you stuck the tip in." Almost breaking out with a smile because of the words I had spoken, however I needed to keep my tough girl façade going so he would take me seriously. "No, I-," I put my hand up cutting him off. "You are going to stick with the lie that you had never seen her before that first night?" "I don't think, so why you are sweating me so hard about this, it's not like that girl is going to die without me." He turned to walk back up the steps to go in his house.

'That girl', is how he referred to my best friend, hell that shit hurt me for her at the time. If I was her, I wouldn't be standing here crying, a brick would have been thrown through his front window. Damn, I knew she was hurting even more after hearing that, but she needed to stop crying so she could see what I was trying to do for her. "Dude, you're a fucking liar". Quan turned around again clearing the steps and proceeded to go in on me.

"Check this out bitch, the only reason I haven't cussed your short ass out is your 'Pop's is my mom's pastor and you're in middle school." He finished breathing hard. I made some mental notes that day, Quan is not sexy when he is mad, he refused to cuss me out because I am the 'pastor's daughter', and because at the time I was in middle school, however he has been knowingly having sex with a girl in middle school. Yep! Quan is a dumbass. Also, I concluded that being a female doesn't mean he will respect me. Eventually I would come to find out just how much he doesn't care about females at all. At least I gained that knowledge about him early on.

To keep from slapping Quan like I watch the pimps do in the movies when their hoes step out of line. I looked around at Quan and Simone's part of the block, it could use some cleaning up, the houses are old. No doubt these houses were probably beautiful when first built, but my dad told me that the 80's drug invasion messed up all places that looked like the 'block'. 4 rows of houses modeled the same inside and out. White miniature 1 story Victorian style houses without the wrap around porches, even the pavement is worn down. Simone's mom makes sure their house is always pressure washed and it's cute inside. In my head the block was put there on purpose to keep the blacks separated from the whites.

I look back up at Quan, again I needed to focus on him and not the fact that if they don't improve the block in 10 years it won't be here, trash is everywhere, the houses are too close together, the kids have no choice but to play in the streets, barely any grass anywhere, it's just wrong. Wrong like the nigga standing in front of me.

"Quan facts are facts, you've been fucking a girl in middle school, age wise you're only two years older than she is, (not justifying the sex) it just looks off because she is in middle school. I call bullshit on the first time you saw Simone was at that party." Exerting the same energy in my voice as he had when he felt the need to call me a 'bitch'. "How you figure that though?" He smiles at me like he can't be proved wrong, confirming for a second time that day he is an idiot. I shook my head, "Nigga, she lives three houses down from you on the same side of the street and with your house being closer to the end of the sidewalk, at the least she passes by your house twice a day, Quan did you grow up in this house?" I asked almost out of breath and patience, he nodded yes. "Then it would be almost impossible that you never saw her." I crossed my arms over my chest, because my point had been made, also I was pissed at Simone still standing there crying. I gave myself a round of applause in my head, I started to think about law school.

Now Quan could walk away or stand on his actions. He closed his eyes putting his head down. As he looked up, Simone's presence was finally acknowledged by him. He walked over and grabs Simon's hand, "I'm sorry", kissing her hand holding him. "I want to rock with you, I know I hurt you, but this wouldn't be a good look for me with you being in middle school. He paused then gave her a weird lop-sided smirk. "Maybe we can work something out. "Work something out? You want her to be your secret, you have us both messed up, let's go Simone!" I snatched Simone's hand out of his, but this chick snatched away from me. I almost slapped the shit out of her from reflex, instead I watched and listened, because I wanted to see how she would respond to whatever Quan offered.

"How can we work anything out Quan, you let me go like I meant nothing to you, and you know that I never lied to you." Her voice low and raspy from all those damn tears. I've never been a heartless person, I felt sorry for my friend, however if that kind of drama comes with having a boyfriend or trying to keep one. I won't rush the process. Whoever I choose has to be worth it, my dad may be right, when you have sex, you are exchanging spirits and God forbid you add bootleg love. That's when you become blinded, that day I witnessed how blinding it can be.

Quan kissed Simone on the forehead and whispered something in her ear. I still don't know what he said to her, but it turned her frown into a smile. Quan turned to go in his house for the third time, he paused, turning around and directing his attention towards me. "For you to be the 'pastors' daughter', you have a filthy mouth, but it's cute." "I refer to it as a colorful, probably why you think it's cute, I heard you

9

do filthy things with your mouth as well Cedrick." I gave him a quick wink, before he had a chance to respond, which he would have if I hadn't grabbed Simone's hand and turned towards her house, that time she didn't resist, and we headed back to her house.

Quan looks as if he is one of those guys that prefer to be called by their street names, but he called me the 'pastor's daughter' as if him calling me that was going to make me mad. We got to Simone's front door I stopped at her doorway, letting her know that my Grandma Eve was in town. So, I needed to head home, as I was turning around to leave, she grabbed my hand. "I love you chick." She told me. I knew she meant it. "I love you too." I headed home mentally exhausted. Honestly, I must admit that day after confronting Quan, I felt somehow as if I had accomplished a situation without swinging, which means that if I try hard enough, I can fight with my words.

On our first day of our freshman year, Quan and Simone became exclusive, however their relationship has been a shit show that I am personally tired of watching.

****

CHAPTER 2

Earlier that day after cheerleading practice I saw Quan picking up the captain of the J.V. Squad Kyomi. Kyomi and I at one point we were close associates, then when we came back to school after summer break, she came to practice with a stank attitude and has kept it ever since. I told my dad about it, because honestly it did brother me. "Babygirl, nothing comes out of nowhere, this may bother you today, and it's okay to wonder why she's giving you an attitude, just pray for her tonight, and trust the Lord to guide you to eventually get clarity on the situation." He spoke.

My dad was right I prayed for her that night, then made a mental note not to care about someone having a problem with me. The problem is inside Kyomi, so it's not my business, however if she ever gets brave enough to try to solve that problem outside of herself. I will be more than happy to assist her.

Kyomi's older sister Tynesha is the captain of the of the Varsity cheer squad, she hates me, but I'm not sure when and why that started, because I've never spoken to her. The beginning of this school year is when I started experiencing the hate from her, basically that's when her little sister started with her attitude, maybe the sisters randomly choose one chick to dislike together every school year. Tynesha expresses it with slick comments behind my back. I pray sometimes that she will do or say the words to my face, that I feel is crossing one of my boundaries, which means if she says anything to me, I'm going to beat her up. A girl can only dream for a moment such as that.

If Simone would get out of her head, I can tell her what I peeped earlier, unfortunately when she gets in this mood there is really nothing that I can say or do. She gets tunnel vision when it comes to Quan, I'm going to tell her what I saw, but I'm hoping someone else witnessed what I did earlier today after practice. That way I won't be adding more fuel to a fire.

Unity is a small town, we have all the ingredients to call it a town, but no matter the size, it doesn't mean that every area is safe to be in after dark. Hopefully, this study session ends before night falls. I got distracted looking back to see how far we have walked from Simone's house, and I accidentally bump into Simone. Thankfully the bump even though it happens on accident seems to bring Simone back to reality. She turns around her eyes are bright she looks down at me and says, "look when we get in here just be yourself, we will be junior's next year, so now is the time to start taking over shit, and I refuse to do all that by myself." Her smile fades as quick as it appears.

Damn, I now know for sure whatever Quan did this time has to be bad, like we might have to kill this nigga bad, and I'm down with that.

Simone is standing here looking at the front door of this house that I've never been to, because it's on the fourth street of the 'block', and I don't know anyone that lives on this street. From the way she is looking I guess we have reached our destination. This house looks like all the other houses on the 'block', however it's bigger the porch is a wrap around, and there is yard space. I have no clue who lives here. I begin to look around to see if I recognize any of the cars randomly parked in the yard. My heart begins to race when I spot Tynesha's car parked next to the red BMW under the carport, if she is here, I know her sister Kyomi is too. I recognize most of the vehicles, and begin to tense up, which causes me to wise up, because this is not a study session.

Locking eyes on the red BMW underneath the carport, makes me question could this be where he lives, of course it is Tynesha is his girlfriend or as she often reminds everyone they are 'high school' sweethearts. Seeing his car is starting to make my body hot, hell seeing him at school drives me crazy. I know that he doesn't notice me, and why should he? Tynesha is a bitch, but no one can deny that she is gorgeous.

Hearing my grandma's voice in my head, 'follow your mind, because your heart can be deceiving and lead you into places with people that mean you no good'. In 'this moment, my mind is screaming for me to go home, I need to just turn around and go home. My heart is pleading with me to stay, just to be in his presence, although he still may not notice that I'm in there. I will still be able to be in his presence. The other people in there, that don't like me for no reason are distractions, and I'm good at tuning people out that hold no importance to me.

It hit me that I can just see him at school, so home is where I need to go. Opening my mouth to let Simone know I've changed my mind and not feeling this whole situation. She begins to walk up to the house and up the stairs leading to the porch. She turns to make sure I'm behind her and says, "I pinky promise this will be fun." I can tell by the look on her face it's not going to be fun.

"Friend, I came to hang out with you not come to a mini-party on a Tuesday." I'm hoping she hears the desperation in my voice of wanting to leave, "also I don't care if anyone behind this door likes me." I say with an attitude but continue follow her up the stairs. Taking a deep breath, "I'm only going in here for you." I grab her hand giving it a light squeeze, as she about to knock on the door I look over at her and say, "I saw Quan and Kyomi together after practice today." We stand there for a while, however in moments like this, that can make it feel as if time has stopped for the information to sink in.

I can feel Simone's anger flowing from her hand to mine. Causing my mind to go into what could possibly take place once we get on the other side of this door. My prayers may be getting answered in a way, however the enemy has to add confusion. Although God does not partake in foolery or the violence I have in mind but I'm thankful for the opportunity I have been given to be around him.

"I love you chick." Simone says to me in a whisper. "I love you too." Simone begins to start knocking on the door like the police.

PRESENT DAY: UNITY POLICE STATION 2004

"Ma'am?" I remove my focus from the ceiling, and my eyes land on a cute young white deputy standing in front of me, which is unusual here in Unity, I see times are changing. "The Chief would like to have a word with you." "Okay." Is my response holding up the wrist that is cuffed to the arm of the chair I'm sitting in. Mrs. Suthers made a dramatic exit earlier when the Chief arrived back to the station. She made sure to loudly and rudely inform the Chief of the reason I am here at the station and requested that I be put in a cell.

Also, she found it necessary to keep saying, "I know her father is rolling over in his grave and that's what he gets for not allowing a woman in his life to teach her better!" As she was yelling at the Chief, I was holding in my laughter, by pursing my lips together, because I didn't want my laughter to be confused with the foolery she was yelling and me shooting my husband. The laughter I was holding back was me wondering how many times during her 'private sessions' with my dad, did those words about me not having a mother were said to try and convince him she could fill that mother role, but I digress.

The young deputy starts to fumble with his keys, I assume he's looking for the cuff key, maybe his nerves are causing him to overlook it. The radio on his hip starts to go off, half a second later the phones at the front desk start to ring back-to-back the deputy looks at the desk behind him where the constant ringing is coming from, then looks back at me. I lift my wrist giving him a reminder that I'm not going anywhere. He rushes to the desk and begins to answer the phones as best as he can by himself.

Why would the Chief want to speak to me? He knows I'm not saying anything without a lawyer present. I feel bad for the Chief, he and my dad were close friends, and he took my father's death hard, and still is having a hard time. It's only been five months. The Chief had been at my house yesterday to give me somewhat of an update on the investigation pertaining to my dad, however he still had no real leads.

I know that he is in a mindset of disappointment with me right now, and I totally understand why he would be. However, I am not sorry for shooting the enemy. I should have thought this turning myself in thing through. I should have gone home first to change into something more comfortable, because this evening gown is not the business.

The deputy spoke in a low voice with each call, after he hung up with the last call, he rushes to the Chief's office in the back. I remember its location, because the last time I was here, my dad and I were filing a sexual complaint leading to a restraining order against my ex-boyfriend Brantley. I was 17 at the time.

"There's been a crash!" the deputy sounds like his nerves are getting the best of him. A few seconds later the deputy and Chief Combs come rushing out. I have always called him Uncle Harry, but I know things will be different from this night on. He turns to look down at me, with disappointment in his eyes. I give him the usual wink as always. We both know that he must leave, under the circumstances I understand his dilemma right now. Breaking the silence I say, "I'll be here when you get back, I promise." Making sure I hold eye contact with my words. He says nothing, just turns and exits the building. I say a silent prayer in my head that no one is hurt in the crash, car wrecks are rare in our little town.

A crash. I direct my attention back to the ceiling. A lot of crashes happened after Simone started pounding on that door.

CHAPTER 3

Knowing that this door Simone is pounding on belongs to the guy of my dreams, is making my nerves bad, however she seems comfortable pounding on the door, so I relax a little. "Who in the fuck knocking on my door like that?" I hear the dude's voice coming from the other side of the door. "Open the door nigga!" Simone yells back. Laughter comes from the dude. "Quan your girl here." Then I hear an eruption of laughter from the other side of the door. All this laughing is starting to piss me off. Simone being upset is not funny to me at all, however if this is how she usually shows up here I can understand how they all may think it's funny. However, I don't find anything amusing.

"Hurry up!" Simone is not letting up on the knocking. "Damn shortie, let me unlock the door." I hear jingles and twisting noises; this place is on lock for real. My dad has us on lock with this high-tech new security system at our house too, so I get it. We use codes, no keys, starting at the front gate, the front door, and any other way you can gain entrance into the house. He says, "if a person doesn't know the code, they have no business at our house." I completely agree with him. Also, my dad loves to be extra and a security system in 1994 in this small town is over the top.

The front door swings open, "move punk!" Simone says shoulder checking the guy that opens the door as she walks pass him. The guy is not just any guy, he's 'the guy', the only guy I want, however this guy is already taken. Unity High does not have a shortage of handsome guys, and sometimes I flirt, however that's about as far as it goes, well until last summer. I haven't had my first kiss yet. I made a connection with a dude, and we almost shared a kiss. We might as well should have, due to the position we were in.

"Here she comes Quan, you better run homie!" he yells back in the house his voice deep and holding amusement. He's bounced back from the shoulder bump Simone had given him, by sweeping off his shoulder as if it had dirt on it. He's still holding a grin looking pass me, I did move to the side as Simone was pounding on the door. I can feel the moisture start to form in between my legs, my body is on fire, and he's just standing there. I must play this situation smooth or I'm going to come off as a weirdo.

I pretend to clear my throat. "Oh, shit I didn't see you standing over there cutie." He bites his bottom lip, looking me up and down. My gaze stays on him, he has what my grandma describes as 'bedroom eyes'. Thick eyebrows, long lashes, and I can only describe his eye color as black, because there is just darkness in them as if he can see your soul. Stepping out on the porch he closes the door behind him as if he isn't planning on inviting me in.

He walks towards me causing me to acknowledge the height difference, He starts to circle around me, I stay still, I hear him repeating, "my, my, my." Smacking his lips as if I'm a meal. Personally, I believe guys think this form of examination is both sexy and intimidating, however it's lame. This dude gets a pass, since the first day I saw him my freshman year I've been wanting him to examine and explore me.

I'm in all black per usual, I didn't have time to change after cheer practice and my cheer shorts leave little to the imagination. I know that my pussy print is visible. Unlike most teen girls my age who make it a mission to point out the problems with their bodies or face. I love everything about me, my grandma says, "you must age gracefully and be grateful at every age, but if you are ungrateful that's when you will start to judge yourself and ignore the beauty has God blessed you with." I'm 5'2, dark chestnut skin I inherited from my dad, my eyes are an almond shape, light hazel eye color, high cheek bones, my nose fits my face perfectly, cute full lips, and a bright smile. My weight stays between 115 to 120lbs it's healthy weight for my height, it's portioned out evenly. Now my hair is a different story my mom and dad both originate out of Louisiana, because of the skin tone difference my dad of darker complexion is what they call Macaroon, my mom is referred to as Mulatto for the lightness of her skin.

On her pictures she looks as if she could have passed for a white woman, however her hair texture would have been a dead giveaway. Fortunately, I inherited everything from her except my skin color, but I love my dark skin. The blacker the berry the sweeter the juice. My hair is big and wavy it doesn't tangle or nap up on me. When I wear it down, which is rare it stops at the mid-section of my back. Majority of the time I keep it up in a bun and depending on the day or the time of the day it may be neat, but most of the time it is messy. Right now, it's messy, because of cheer practice. I have on an all-black Adidas pullover with the white stripes, my shoes match my hoodie.

My Grandma Eve complains about the way that I dress, "Why do you dress like you are heading for a brawl?" I laugh when she asks that, I understand her question, because she is partly right, because you never know when something crazy might pop off. I describe my style as 'sexy and comfortable'. I believe no matter what you wear you either have it or you don't, and from the way this dude is checking me out 'I have it'.

I can't count how many times I've laid in my bed and dreamt of a moment to be this close to him. I need to stay focused. I can do this. "You done?" I ask looking up at him with a straight face, once he's back in front of me. "My bad sweetie, I was just admiring you, I'm not sure if we've seen you before." He gives me a smile cocking his head to the side. I decide it's my turn to check him out. His simple style of dress is sexy. White wife beater, purple basketball shorts, white footie socks, and black Nike slides. I look back up into his eyes. "Maybe you don't look around enough, I see you at school," hoping he doesn't hear the quavering in my voice from my nervousness. I wonder if he can hear my heart beating, because I can. I need to be present in this moment, because a moment like this may never happen again, he smells so good though. I want to grab and kiss him.

"Well let me introduce myself so when you see me you can say 'hey' sometimes, my name is Genesis." Holding his hand out, "I'm pretty sure everyone knows your name." I state, taking his hand. "Word! Yet I've never heard it come out of your mouth." "Nope, you haven't, because I don't conversate or touch other people's property." Removing my hand from his.

Genesis Montreal Lucas is the starting quarterback of our Varsity football team, a senior with unlimited college offers, and the boyfriend of Tynesha. Rumor has it and in small towns most rumors stem form a little truth. Genesis may flirt but, he is said to be faithful and loyal to his girlfriend. Unfortunately, on the other hand Tynesha doesn't hold the same values in their relationship as him.

I held witness to that myself with my own eyes. Both J.V. and Varsity football teams had a pre-season game with our rival team Pratt High, the next town over on the same night. I forgot my pom-poms on the bus, when I went back to retrieve them, at the back of the bus Tynesha was on her knees going to work on the J.V.'s starting quarterback Brantley who was a freshman at the time but wasn't playing that night due to an injury. However, I could tell by his moaning and the quick, glance I got of him the injury didn't involve his dick. I know of the guy and have seen him at a few revivals, that she was servicing, because his dad is also a pastor, so if churches had rivalries his dad and my dad are enemies. When I saw what was going on I didn't act startled or surprised, I grabbed my pom-poms and made my exit off the bus. Brantley is a cute guy, but if I was to cheat on Genesis, hold up I wouldn't cheat on Genesis.

Quan and Genesis are best friends, so I didn't tell Simone what I saw that night, because I know she would have told Quan. Even if she would have made him promise not to tell I'm sure he would have put his best friend up on game the same way that she and I do with each other.

I could have been in Genesis' presence before today, however that would require being around Quan and Simone all the time and I can't handle that. That's why my prayers have been to set it up the way He (God) sees fit. Therefore, if it were ever going to happen, I wanted it to be set up by God.

Being a cheerleader is an outlet for me, however this season we have been working with the Varsity cheer squad more, so I get to see Genesis more often, because the Varsity cheerleaders practice within eyesight of the football teams after practice, even if he is with her. I know it's probably in my head, but I swear I can feel him watching me sometimes. Football games are an added requirement, I honestly couldn't tell you the first thing about football. My dad said I had to participate in one extra-curricular activity and I'm pretty good at cheer. The girls on the squad aren't my friends, I call them 'friendly associates'. My dad is satisfied with the choice I made to become a cheerleader and I am too. It was either be a cheerleader or be at the church 24/7.

Simone is the only person that I have openly expressed my undying love for Genesis to, other than my journals. She is sworn to secrecy, even though I know she and Quan have a 'no secrets policy' in their relationship. Which Quan breaks every time he cheats and lies about it.

She wouldn't throw me under the bus with that information, at least I hope not.

Genesis' mom is another devoted member at our church, he only attends with her on the holiday services. I always feel excitement when I look down from the balcony and see him. "You look familiar," he pauses and squints his eyes as if that will help him see me better. "Oh shit, you're the 'pastor's daughter." "Yep. That's me." I say holding my right thumb up to let him know he is correct. Hearing him call me that stings, because contrary to popular belief, I do have a name. "Wait! Simone is your homegirl?" he asks, and I can tell he is trying to make the connection with us being friends. Understandable. "More like sisters, I just don't come around much." Hearing him mention Simone's name helps me remember why and who I am here for and that's her. "I see." He says, licking those sexy lips again and crossing his arms across his chest. His lips alone, I am sure can satisfy both sets of my lips. I may not know exactly what to do with him, but I'm a quick learner and he is probably a good teacher.

Genesis' skin is a dark caramel complexion he has the body of your typical high school athlete, but times two! Noticeable muscles, body ripped just right, it's his eyes, however his eyes hold all his greatness, at least to me. Even looking up into them right now, they hold so much enchantment. I wonder what he really sees, I bet that he's a deep and big thinker in placed in small town. He stands a good 6'1, at school I love watching the way he walks, my grandma told me you can tell a lot about a man by the way he walks. If her theory is true Genesis walks as if he knows his presence is both powerful and a gift. If he licks those lips like LL Cool J, I'm going to believe that 'he needs love'. I'll have to pull him down or get up on my tiptoes, either way a kiss is going to happen, then I'll ask if he wants to come over later, my dad left this morning for two weeks for a 'church conference' in Louisiana. I'm home alone.

There is no doubt, he can have any girl at the school, any chick out of school, hell he can have any chick that's alive his options are unlimited. School politics are important at Unity High School, as I imagine they are at all schools. Tynesha and Genesis are a beautiful couple look wise, she is tall Coke bottle shape, she has that exotic look going on, and her features stand out I bet she has a lot of Native blood in her. Her hair is dyed honey blonde, cut short and compliments her face. Look wise she is beautiful it's her insides take away from her beauty, That's just my opinion. Kyomi her little sister not only looks, but acts like her, Kyomi's body is not as developed yet, her skin tone is a shade darker, but instead of honey blonde hair she rocks jet black hair in the same short style.

"So, you're not down with OPP?" letting his words flow out like he is a part of the rap group "Naughty by Nature'." "No, I don't share." I smile and get up on my tiptoes trying to look over his shoulder, knowing I will only be looking at a closed door. I make the motion to get closer to him as well, while also reminding him the person who I came here with is on the other side of the door. Hopefully, she is not in there acting like a nutcase.

"Are you going to let me in I need to check on Simone" I adjust my bookbag from one shoulder to the other, because it does have books in it, reason being this is supposed to be a 'study session'. He turns around heading for the front door, midway he spins around causing me to flinch, our bodies are almost touching. He's hovering over me, I look up at him holding eye contact my body is getting hot, my heart rate is speeding up, and my pussy is throbbing as if calling for him. However, I'm not uncomfortable, Genesis runs his right hand slowly and gently across my left chick as if he is making sure that I'm real. "What's your name?" he asks in a low tone. His breathing is heavy. "Merci."

The longer he keeps his hand on my cheek, the harder it gets for me to stand, my legs are starting to feel like Jell-O. Then it hits me this is the feeling people get at Michael Jackson concerts, I need to ask God to forgive me for judging those people. I understand now when you care for a person, it doesn't matter if you know them or not it's how that person makes you feel up close or far apart.

CHAPTER 4

"**N**igga! I will fuck all this shit up if you don't stop lying!" I hear my best friend's voice clearly through the door, breaking the connection between Genesis and me. Have we been so caught up into each other that we tuned everything and everyone out?" We both give a deep sigh. I know that I need to go check on Simone and depending on how the situation is when I get inside, I might have to check on and check his best friend as well. Opening the front door Genesis lets me know that I can place my bookbag down by a small table next to the front door. "Thanks." I say walking pass him not knowing where to go, I just let Simon's voice guide me to her.

I enter what looks to may have once been a family room, does Genesis live here alone? The room is giving me bachelor pad vibes, I stop just pass the archway observing the room, not the people. My dad says, "always observe everything in a room you are in, then observe the people in the room." "Oh snap! Who do we have here? I know it's not the 'pastor's daughter!'" Tynesha asks and answers her question loudly. However, I hear the surprise in her voice, probably because she never thought I would ever be in the same place as her. I squint my eyes at her, I really don't have to be here and instead of wasting time, I should just snatch her up and leave.

While gazing at her thinking whether if I should just beat her ass and leave, I flinch feeling a light graze across the small of my back, "let me get by you sexy," Genesis says softly. I decide to stay and see where this evening might lead. I'm looking at his bitch and she is looking at me, however I can see the unknown hatred she has for me in her face. If this is a staring contest, I'm going to win, I hate losing at anything, also the prize might be her boyfriend.

"Who is the bitch Quan?" Damn it! Simone's voice messes up another moment that could have led to something great for me.. Why is she asking who the bitch is when I already told her? The feeling that is beginning to form in my gut is letting me know that this evening is going to be nothing less than interesting. My intuition in rarely off, because my spirit is still telling me to get the hell out of this house. I'm going to stay though, but I'll pay extra attention to whatever is going on. Grandma Eve says, "you need to go through situations to have good stories to tell your grandchildren, they will enjoy, learn and know it's okay to live, because of those stories. I wonder how much I will learn while I'm here. After whatever that was that happened on the porch between Genesis and myself, I have no doubt I want him, also I have no doubt in my heart I know this evening Tynesha will learn by my words or by the laying of hands that I am not the one.

I peep the toxic couple Simone and Quan in a corner of the family room. I approach with caution, reason being Simone's anger can go either way depending on the depth of the situation. Quan not answering her question that she has probably asked an unimaginable number of times by now makes it worse. I assume Simone is in her 'I don't give a fuck' phase. Approaching her with caution I touch her arm, "friend why did you leave me?" I'm intentionally trying to sound as if I care she left me on the porch, I'm reaching with the question. Thank God it works a little, not much, but enough to feel some of the tension leave her body. Simone looks back at Quan tensing back up, "plus you and I both know anger brings premature wrinkles, Grandma Eve would be upset with you if she were here, especially knowing you are risking your beauty on a nigga that isn't worth it." Calm down.

I mention my grandma, during times such as this, when Simone gets in this mood. My grandma is a small substitute as a mom Simone and myself. I must give it to my grandma she gives the best advice, she is the true definition of 'sugar, spice, and everything nice'. Simone adores her and cherishes her words of wisdom as much as I do.

My words work Simone's shoulders relax. "Yeah, listen to Merci, except that I'm not worth it shit." Quan says quietly. We both look at him, "you need to shut the fuck up!" we say in unison. Being friends for as long as we have Simone and I often speak at the same time, we've gotten used to this. Turning around I realize our meeting in the corner wasn't private, faces are looking at us and the room full of teenagers is silent. Quan slips away during the moment of silence. His timing is perfect, the people in the room are staring at Simone and me. Another staring match, I hate losing, but this one is uncomfortable, so I'll take this loss.

Eventually, the stare down ends. The room becomes active again, I grab Simone's hand giving it an extra squeeze, I have a suggestion, she has to lean down a little for me to be able to whisper it in her ear. "You got this, we got this, high-key on a real tip I think that we should turn this study session into our kind of fun, I feel in my spirit that is my real purpose for being here," I giggle trying to tell her what I want. "You may be right best friend." Her voice is easy, which makes me feel like if I had gone home, her disagreement with Quan may not have ended in her favor. Excitement fills up in my heart, because we are both in agreeance about having our kind of fun. Our version of fun is full of pettiness and usually ends in violence, I'm okay with this. "I'll let you know when it's time to 'dance'", I say 'dance' instead of fight, it gives it a more dramatic feel. "Cool" is Simone's response followed by a smile.

"Now, let's go join the rest of your crew." I say sarcastically, still holding her hand she leads me in the direction of her people she hangs with outside of me. People I know, but not on a personal level. All of them I see at school and some of them at church. I keep in mind that first impressions set the tone, although I attend school with all of them, this is going to be my first, "hey, guys I'm Merci." Not the 'pastor's daughter' impression. Truthfully, as I look around I can careless if my impression is good or bad, all I know is it will be an impression that everyone in this house will remember.

CHAPTER 5

I take a seat next to Simone on a love seat, directly across from the sisters. Genesis is sitting in between them closer to Tynesha. Quan appears out of nowhere and sits in a chair that looks like it once belonged to a dining room set next to Simone. He's whispering to her, it's crazy Quan doesn't have anything to say when she asks him about the chicks he gets caught with, but he has plenty to say when he wants forgiveness. She's tuning him out. I'm going to get us a soda my mouth is dry." Simone says standing up and walks away. I hate when she does the abrupt walking away thing, especially right now, because she's heading to get beverages and has now made it impossible for me to ask the drink options.

"Merci, can you please calm her down?" I refuse to look at Quan. Rolling my eyes, landing them on the ceiling. "Quan who did you pick up earlier today? That I would have seen, because you make sloppy moves?" Taking my eyes off the ceiling and letting my eyes land on Kyomi with a big grin, cocking my head to the side. "You really need to be more careful dude or by now know how make smarter moves."

"You snitched me out? Damn it's like that?" He's not speaking in a low tone now, it seems he want to project his anger towards me, by getting loud, however it's not working.

Quan and I turn our heads towards the direction of where the laughing is coming from, Genesis is looking at us with a grin on his face, obviously he has been eavesdropping on our conversation. I know that it's just my hormones that have me hot right now, by looking at him. I know asking if anyone else is hot won't make sense. However, this isn't a moment to enjoy how sexy Genesis' is even when he laughs, because this situation and conversation isn't something to be amused about. Quan wants to plead his case to me. I've already spilled the beans and I have no intentions of picking them up. "Just keep me out of it, she already knew something was up, I only gave the name of who I saw you with, that way she would be in the know." Quan's confusion about me telling on him is starting to confuse me.

I'm ready for Quan to graduate, hopefully he will find a chick in college. I know that will break Simone's heart, but the drama will stop. I pray her next dude she falls for is an angel, but if she stays with Quan, he needs to know I'm snitching it's not personal, because that applies to whoever she is in a relationship with. When I start dating, I know that she will do the same for me.

"That's dirty man," Quan is being overly dramatic, and it's weird, he is acting as if this the first time he's messed up or I've had to hurt Simone's feelings, by relaying information about him being wreckless with his dick. "Dirty! How do you figure that? I don't owe you any loyalty, you made the dumb choice of picking Kyomi up, I saw it and what Simone does with that information are the consequences of your dumb ass choice." I speak loudly on purpose, reason being I want Kyomi to hear me as well. Feeling Genesis' eyes on me so I look at him and remember that he is half of the reason that I haven't left, because we've been here about 20 minutes and I'm ready to go.

"Excuse me 'church girl' did you say my name?" Kyomi asks chewing the gum in her mouth making sure to add that annoying popping noise. Again, contrary to popular belief, I do not mind being called 'church girl' or the 'pastor's daughter'. My dad is an amazing pastor, so I really feel a sense of pride in that, my dad owns his church literally, but he does not make it an obligation for me to be at the church or attend church on the regular. Yeah, I'm a church girl, a pastor's daughter, and a proud daddy's girl. Kyomi should come to church, maybe at some point this evening I will invite her and Tynesha to morning service on Sunday. "Yes, captain I did." I answer feeling my sarcasm start to kick up a notch. "Quan and I were discussing him picking you up after practice earlier and there could possibly be a mix up. I personally want to believe he was picking you up as an act of kindness, however his girlfriend who is my best friend, well she believes you two were pulling a 'hoe move', with us all being in the same room," I wave my hand around to emphasize the 'us all being in the same room' part, "hopefully we can get some clarification and Simone can get a clear explanation, then she can decide whether it was an act of kindness or a 'hoe move'." My dad would be so impressed if he were here right now, I only use the sweet southern accent when his friends come to visit. It's also the accent I use to belittle ignorant people, getting loud is not my style.

I sit back further on the love seat folding my arms across my chest, crossing my right leg over my left, then look up at the ceiling tracing the pattern with my eyes. I wonder why this house is bigger than the others on the 'block'? Simone is taking forever with those drinks, which means there are options if it's taking her this long.

A bright light blasts on, revealing the darker spots in the room, revealing people who've obviously been hiding in the darkness. "Hey, Gen' can we shoot a game of pool?" I recognize the dude asking the question and the others standing around waiting for an answer from school. Genesis throws his hands up, signaling that it's cool. There is no doubt in my head that Genesis lives here alone, maybe he has an agreement with his mom.

"She doesn't need to clarify or give anyone an understanding about anything I gave the girl a ride home nothing happened," Quan sounds mad, and I don't give a shit if he is. I give a one shoulder shrug with my left shoulder. "The thing is Cedrick if that is true then your story and her story of what happened earlier should match perfectly." I gaze at him only, making sure Kyomi feels that in this moment she doesn't matter, her story won't matter to Simone anyway, like my Grandma Eve says, "it's called 'History' for a reason, the woman's story doesn't matter. I refuse to break eye contact with Quan, he can get as aggressive and pretend as if he is going to turn into the 'Incredible Hulk' all he wants. How many times do I have to a remind a person they are not God? Point being I don't fear Quan, I think he is hilarious, but that is about it. Nothing more. Nothing less.

"What do you mean?" Tynesha asks and for some reason her voice always sounds like nails on a chalkboard. I take a deep breath to keep from snatching her up, "where did I lose you in what I said to your sister and Quan? I'm sure I can help find you wherever you got lost." I sit up from the position I had been sitting in, so she can understand through my body language, to let her know that backhand bullshit she has been pulling at school, won't be taking place at this 'study session! This old coffee table is the only thing between she and I.

"Don't talk to my sister like she's dumb!" Kyomi always wants to defend her big sister, Simone and I defend each other, in a way I can appreciate that about her, and I understand, however I don't care for either of these bitches. "Are you going to make me stop talking to her like that?" I can feel the evil smirk forming on my face. Shifting my body to face Kyomi anxiously waiting for her to answer.

"Hold up! Hold up, What's the beef?" Genesis' sits up. He's looking at me for answers, his eyes still holding lust, but I can tell he is thrown off by the conversation and the tension that is present between the sisters and me. "The beef is I'm sick of these hoes trying my man!" Simone answers his question loudly, causing me to look up in surprise. As she takes her seat beside me holding my favorite strawberry soda. This is what I believe to be perfect timing. "Okay, but who are the hoes?" Genesis asks. Is he being serious right now? His face is full of curiosity, crazy that he doesn't know the answer to his own question. "Both of them!" Simone and I say in unison for the second time this evening, Simone's finger points towards Kyomi and mine to Tynesha, our in-sync actions surprising us this time. We look at each other and burst out in laughter, then the room erupts in laughter. The only people in the room not laughing are Genesis and the sisters.

When I see Genesis is not laughing, but looking at me squinting his thick eyebrows together, biting his bottom lip, it's not holding that sexiness as it did a minute ago. He's holding a "that shit isn't funny" gaze. Still looking at me he sits back further on the sofa he is on with the sisters, puts his arm around Tynesha then pulls her in closer. He believes pulling his girlfriend close to him is something that bothers me, he's thinking too much of himself because I see them hugged up at school every day.

I give him a lop-side smirk, open my soda, and take a sip. I refuse to believe that at no place or time Genesis doesn't know his girlfriend gives it out to other guys. Why is he offended by it now?

To appear as if I am not paying attention to Genesis affection to his girlfriend, because the room is still full of laughter. I decide now is the time to check out the scenery a little more. I peep over at Quan still holding the look of distraught on his face, "nigga please." I whisper to myself. Cedrick "Quan" Banks is the definition of 'sexual chocolate', the danger in that is Quan knows he's sexy, he also knows the girls think about him the same way, that he thinks of himself. Therefore, his ego feeds on that knowledge, Quan uses his looks every chance given. Simone will eventually move on. I only tolerate him because of her. I do see him looking at my best friend sometimes and not even I can deny he has love for her, that's another reason I put up with him.

I look over towards the pool table randomly placed in the living room, making it crystal clear in my head that Genesis lives here alone. "Merci, damn it's about time, you finally made the decision to join us!" Gabe's voice sends a tingle down my spine. "Dude, I didn't see ya'll sitting there!" I say happily, I'm not thrown off, because why wouldn't they be here. I have to say 'ya'll' even though only one voice spoke to me. I can't control my smile as I get up to hug Gabe and his identical twin brother Mike, who's sitting next to him smiling like a Cheshire cat. I allow the grin to stay on my face, because I'm happy that I have people in this room I know other than Simone.

The twins and I don't talk to each other at school, if we do it's a simple 'hey'. Other than Simone, Gabriel and Michael are two people I consider friends, by way of my dad's church. Basically, they are 'church boys', well in the presence of their mom and my dad. They both heavily resemble the actor Allan Payne, just younger versions and more muscular bodies. I have to take a deep breath every time I see them with their shirts off. Light skin, black curly hair with a tight edge, big plush pink lips, sleepy eyes, they are Seniors along with Genesis and Quan, also our two starting wide receivers on the Varsity football team

Their mother is another devoted member in and out of church to my dad. My dad took on being their mentor, due to the absence of their own father, and I get that. However, my father is a pastor and I have a lot more freedom than the twins. I bet they had to tell their mom this is a 'study session' for them to be here.

Gabe and Mike are alike in so many ways other than them being identical. Twins usually go in the 'good and bad' categories. In my opinion Gabe is the good one and Mike is the bad one. I'm closer to Gabe, Mike scares me sometimes with his words. It's open knowledge that they have this crazy rule that if you date one you date the other as well and I've seen that foolery with my own eyes. I only know of one girl Gabe has kept away from Mike, and I question that, however his secret is safe with me. Well-behaved is how they are when their mom is around, now I get the chance to see their behavior with their crew, outside of church and school. This should be enlightening.

"Ya'll know shortie?" Genesis asks as I'm sitting back down from embracing the twins with hugs. I'm acting as if I didn't feel Gabe pull me in closer and tighter than he usually does on a Sunday morning, probably because our bond changed in a major way over the summer. "Yeah, we are basically family." Mike answers throwing a peanut at me playfully, I dodge out of the way, genuinely laughing at his action with love.

I catch Simone looking at me with a smirk, quickly giving me a heads up and a side eye towards Genesis. "Why haven't ya'll ever brought her to hangout?" Silence enters our space in the room at the question. Genesis can't get his answer because Tynesha speaks up with her own question. "Why do you care who she knows or why she hasn't been here?". She slides away from him showing her annoyance by folding her arms across her chest.

CHAPTER 6

"It really doesn't matter why she is here. We are happy she's here." Mike states holding a smirk, then takes a sip from his cup. Gabe says nothing. However, he holds up his Sprite can towards me as if to make a toast openly showing his allegiance to me, and his agreeance with his brother.

"All credit of my presence goes to my bestie right here." I nudge Simone with my elbow, she needs to tune back in and stop shooting daggers into Kyomi with her eyes, she flinches, then touches her soda to mine to finish the toast.

Genesis stays quiet, but is looking at me, I glance over at Gabe who's watching Genesis look at me, from the visible clenching of Gabe's jaw I can tell he doesn't like the attention Genesis is showing me. "Okay, can we get this over with?" Tynesha blurts out looking at me her face holding a sneaky grin as if she knows something I don't and right now she does. "Quick question?" Simone sits up why are you and her here?" looking from Kyomi to Tynesha. "From my understanding ya'll weren't supposed to be here today." I can tell my friend is being serious, but why wouldn't they be here? Genesis clears his throat and looks up at Quan. "Simone, stop." Quan says to her. "Okay, but whatever pops off is your fault." She looks at Quan I can't see her face, but he places his head in his hands, as if he knows that he has messed up.

"Excuse me?" I ask, "Oh, your bestie didn't give you all the information? Honey, you don't get to hangout with us, because you are friends with her, you have to go through our version of initiation." Tynesha is mocking my southern accent that I had used earlier and I'm impressed, because I thought being a bitch and a whore were her only talents.

I give her a grin, that I'm sure resembles a snarl just prettier, but I can't help but to feel I'm being setup with some fuckery. First of all, 'initiation' sounds as if like some cult shit. Yeah, this is my cue to leave. I begin to stand, it's been fun, and I got the opportunity to have a moment with Genesis, so I'm satisfied. "Where are you going?" Simone asks, confusion on her face looking up at me. "Home, I only came because you said this was a 'study session'" I can't finish talking, the room erupts in laughter, Simone included.

I'm not trying to mess anything up with my grades, my dad has promised me a brand-new car for my birthday, and he asked me last month what kind of car I have in mind. Studying and keeping straight A's is high on my list of what I think is important, also my 16th birthday is Friday, and I want my car. I scan the room real quick including my best friend in this observation, and exclude the twins, because their mom is just as concerned about their grades as she is their souls. I conclude that most of the kids in this room keep their grades high enough to participate in sports. Now, I'm in complete understanding my grandma's words, "ignorance is bliss, keep making those good grades in school, you will get to pick the any college you want to and won't have to pay for anything, get a job doing what you want, and never forget it's brains over beauty. A pretty face will get you in the door, but knowledge will keep you in the room.

The room starts to settle down as I sit back down, accepting the fact that I am in a room full of people that will choose popularity over education any day. "Merci." Genesis' voice catches my attention while catching Tynesha's attention as well. I want to smile hearing my name come out of his mouth, I hold a straight face looking at him, and raising my eyebrows signaling that he has my attention and to continue speaking. Genesis holds his hands up, as if he is showing that he means me no harm, "have you ever played the game 'truth or dare'?" "No." I answer. "Okay, to be able to hang with me," he catches his words, but it's too late, we all heard him. Awkward.

Tynesha stands and he snatches her back down, giving her a glare. "I meant to say hang with us, the initiation is just a quick game of 'truth or dare'." I am trying to pay attention and listen to Genesis. However, I keep gazing at Gabe for him to give me a sign to help navigate if I should play or not. Gabe is already looking at me, his face is serious, but he gives me a wink, a silent signal to let me know that everything is cool. Genesis clears his throat, I direct my attention to him, but he is looking at Gabe with annoyance.

"The way we play is you can do one big dare, or you answer 4 questions no matter how personal or crazy you have to answer truthfully." Again, I'm listening to Genesis explaining this childish game, his eyes are intense, then I wonder if the one big dare question might be to kiss him. I glance at Tynesha and doubt that will be the dare. I need to focus.

"She'll take the 4 truth questions, because ya'll go too far with that one dare." Simone decides to choose for me. I take a deep breath making sure she can feel my body inhale and exhale, I am checking her when we leave here. I would never lead her into some bullshit like this. Then again, I can't be mad, she already knew I would have declined the invite if she would have told me the real deal. "I'll be asking the questions!" Tynesha announces loudly and with excitement. I smile at her, because I know she is viewing this as an opportunity to get under my skin, and I'm going to use this as an opportunity to beat her ass.

"Merci, you ready?" Gabe asks, I don't answer him. "Before we start." Mike speaks up his deep voice booming through the room. "We," he points from himself to his brother, "we are not going to let ya'll play with her, so ask the questions and get this over with!" Mike looks at Gabe who nods in agreeance. Gabe looks worried, but it's sexy seeing him worried about me. "I third that." Simone voices, nudging me in the side.

Reality is I could care less about ever hanging out at this house or being around these people in it. I'll see them at school or church and things can stay the same as before I stepped in this house. I'm going to play because I want to show that I'm more than just the 'pastor's daughter', my name is Merci. However, I will show no mercy if Tynesha takes things to far that is when she will learn only God is merciful. I take a sip of my soda, place the can back on the old coffee table and sit back in the love seat trying to get comfortable. The room gets dead silent, as if a storm is brewing. I tap Simone on the leg signaling to her that the 'dance' will start soon.

I take one more deep breath, I look at Tynesha and say, "let the games begin."

CHAPTER 7

Tynesha is about to ask the first question, "Listen, don't ask nothing disrespectful" Simone says loudly not talking to anyone in particular. "Merci looks and acts like she can handle a few questions if not she would have left or you shouldn't have brought her here", Tynesha's voice is full of excitement, she probably has more than four questions to ask the excitement still in her voice is starting to make me worry. It's obvious that she has been waiting for a moment like this with me, the same goes for me, but I know my reason for disliking her. The real question is why she doesn't like me.

"I believe Merci can handle anything." Genesis interrupts the silence. He has everyone's attention especially mine. What and why would he let that come out of his mouth? The look on his face shows that he didn't mean to say those words out loud. However, Tynesha isn't looking at him she is staring at me as if I made her boyfriend say that. I return her stare, but at the same time I know she's more caught off guard than I am.

"No! We are not treating her any different, she is not special. Sis, ask her whatever the fuck you want!" Kyomi is mad, I'm guessing she sees, her sister is shaken up by what Genesis believes I can handle.

I acknowledge Kyomi's words by shrugging my shoulders I know she is trying to protect her sister, while trying to stay relevant, I do look over at Quan and wonder what he was thinking earlier messing with Kyomi. Appearance inside and outside Simone shuts Kyomi or whoever the other hoes have been down, with just her smile. Easily Simone can be a model with her milk chocolate skin, long legs, her eyes have an oval shape that hold a hone-hazel color, her jet black natural thick shoulder length hair, her lips shaped like the real Betty Boop, (who happens to be a black woman) and her dimples when she smiles are the perfect compliment to her beauty. Simone is stacked in all the right places, she can pas for 18 easily. That's why I question Quan's stupidity, because Simone's personality enhances her outside beauty. However, my dad has sex with a lot of different women. Who knows what men really want?

"First question, I'll make it easy. Have you ever been kissed by a boy, like on the lips?" "No." My answer is quick, because it's true, Gabe starts coughing, then he starts choking catching everyone's attention. I know why he is reacting that way, but my answer shouldn't have thrown him off. I assume the lips Tynesha is asking about are the set on my face, Gabe did not kiss those lips. I remember clearly what did and did not take place over the summer at church camp. He and I should probably talk about what happened later. "Bro you, okay?" Genesis asks him. I see Mike patting his brother on the back out the side of my eye, I choose not to look directly at him. "Yeah, I must have swallowed down the wrong hole."

I keep my eyes on the bitch asking the questions. Gabe can choke all he wants. He and I know we didn't kiss. "Next question, please?" I am ready to get this over with. "Are you a virgin?" she asks. She has to be kidding me. I glance around the room making eye contact with no one, because this should have been the first question. I purse my lips together first, then answer, "of course." These are some boring questions. I think if this would be a good time to inform Tynesha that I am waiting to give her boyfriend my virginity as his graduation gift. A riot will come from that, but if the questions stay boring, I will start a riot, this really is a lose-lose situation. She's wasting my time, also who doesn't enjoy a good riot.

I feel Simone nudge me. I lean in to hear her, she whispers in my ear through gritted teeth hiding behind a fake smile, girl look how Genesis is looking at you. I turn my head fast to look back at him, people that are paying attention follow my gaze. Yep! He is looking at me as if we are the only two people in the room. Sucking his bottom lip through his teeth, his eyes seem darker and are piercing through me. Unfortunately, an annoying voice that belongs to a person who wants to stay relevant breaks the connection. "You sure about that?" Kyomi shoots her stupid question out her mouth. I cock my head to the side looking at her with squinted eyes, trying to see why she would ask me anything. "Yes, she's sure, you mad?" Simone gets words out before I can. Again, laughter gives life to the room. I tap Simone on the knee, because I feel the 'dance' is getting close.

"Okay, the shit is not that funny, I'm ready to ask the next question." Tynesha can't be mad at us, because she created that mini version of herself, she should tell Kyomi being a hoe isn't cool. I can feel it, she's really going to give me a reason and opportunity to beat her ass. Look at God! The room begins to settle again, then she asks, "do you think that my boyfriend is fine?" "That's the question?" I ask giggling, to make sure that she and I are both clear on the question. "Yeah, answer my question." She's hungry for my answer, so much so she grabs Genesis' face and starts tonguing him down, adding moans. I look over at Simone we both shrug our shoulders, I feel a tad bit jealous, but Genesis is her boyfriend, she can kiss him anytime she wants. It sucks. However, it's not going to change my answer, and now I have more to add to my answer. I'm glad I mad the decision to come this evening

Finally, the kiss comes to an end, Kyomi fells the need to reach over to give her sister a high five. That's weird, I make a mental note, I've definitely missed something. Why would she basically congratulate her sister for kissing her boyfriend? That's weird.

"So, what's your answer?", "Of course he is fine as hell, we all can see that, I would also like to add from the kiss you just shared with him that he looks as if tastes delicious. Does he taste as delicious as he looks?" I sit up to make my question personal, "Genesis are you as delicious as your girlfriend just made you look during that kiss?" looking at him with a straight face. "My girl said delicious!" Simone yells out, the room explodes with talking, yelling, and laughing. Simone is beside me going crazy. Honestly, I want to show out with my friend, because I'm surprised with myself with everything I said after I answered Tynesha's dumb question. Genesis is looking at me grinning from ear to ear, we stare at each other, until Quan reaches over and gives him dap, Mike and Gabe follow suit dapping him up as well.

I understand that my entire response to Tynesha's question is going to start something, and that was my point of my words, I needed to provoke her to say something that can start the 'dance'. There is no reason to have a 'study session' with teenagers and something doesn't get started. At least that's my belief. I began watching Kyomi and Tynesha quietly talking amongst themselves and their body movements. She and I both know this fourth question she is willing to risk her safety, just to hurt me in some kind of way. She hates me that much and I still don't know why. I nudge Simone with my knee, she looks at me I give her the heads up in the sisters' direction. Knowing that all this sitting around is about to end, and the 'dance' will begin. My gut tells me to grab my soda from the coffee table, I take a sip, but I don't place the can back on the table, my grandma would be proud of me, listening to my 'women's intuition'.

The room becomes silent for the last question my gaze lands on Gabe he knows me, and his face is serious. Mike sits up holding the same seriousness on his face as Gabe, they both know that if this question goes out of bounds it's over. Poor Genesis has no clue what may take place if his girlfriend asks the wrong question, but my dad says there are always casualties in war. Mike clears his voice loudly, I can't help to shoot a look at him and his brother, they both do that 'twin shit' and give a wink in unison with the same eye. "We gave a warning to ya'll about Merci, so whatever happens is on ya'll, carry on." Mike warns Tynesha without looking her way. I position myself towards

Tynesha to have a straight shot at her. Simone has inched closer to me. She'll have a good right hook when she lands on Kyomi.

"Please, don't ask nothing crazy." Quan's voice is pleading with Tynesha. "No! She can handle anything remember?" Kyomi inserts. "Bitch, shut up." Simone's words are cold, letting me know that she is ready to hit the 'dance' floor. I freaking love my best friend. Tynesha sits up to the edge of her seat all teeth showing, communicating with me she is about to attempt to prove that she is 'that bitch'. Lord, bless her heart.

"Is it true that your daddy the pastor, had your mama shot down, because she went to the Feds on him?" she asks sitting back crossing her arms across her chest, as if she knows she's hit her mark. "Tynesha, What the fuck?!" Genesis yells looking at her and pushing her away from him.

****

I watched a crime documentary once and the lady said she committed a 'crime of passion'. That was the description to justify killing her husband and the woman she caught with him in their marital bed. She said the feeling of sadness, rage, betrayal, and also the disrespect flooded her body, but she could still see, however, only in the color red as if her eyes were bleeding from the inside. She continued to say how, she walked to the closet to retrieve the gun, in her mind at the time that was the only logical thing she could think to do.

She shot her husband and his mistress in the head, saying after that everything went black. The police in the documentary said she shot each victim multiple times, however due to the overflow of emotions mixed with adrenaline, caused the lady to black out. Leaving her only to remember the first two shots. The woman didn't get any jail or prison time, because of the whole 'crime of passion' thoery. So, just because she started seeing red, she got away with killing two people. When I watched it, I didn't believe that to be possible. I questioned the seeing red theory. Right now, I know that it's not a theory it's real, because all I can see is red and I all I want to do is kill this bitch.

****

I hear my heart beating in my ear. I feel Simone gripping my thigh, I have tunnel vision, a red tunnel. What did this bitch just ask me? My mom is dead, she died a brutal death, and this bitch asks if my dad had something to do with it" Wow, she truly hates me, and I am clear on that. I don't know what I did for her or her little sister to have this kind of hatred towards me, and at one point I wanted to know why, but from now on I could care less. They will fear me every time they see me. Hopefully, I don't kill this bitch, because I will not show mercy.

I look down at the soda, shit everything is red including the soda can, I'm gripping it tightly in my hand. "Dance!" I yell to give Simone the signal to go, while clearing the table I throw the soda can as hard as possible it connects in the middle of Tynesha's forehead, my fist connects a split second after. Hell is raging inside of me, and I'll be damn, because everything is fading to black.

It's getting chilly in here and this cuff around my wrist is irritating my skin. Being thirsty is an understatement, maybe someone is in here, somewhere, leaving a jail completely unattended should be against the law. I'm going to chance it, may God answer my prayer by sending an angel, or a deputy in the back may be able to hear me. "Hello! Is anyone in here." I yell not expecting an answer and hoping they didn't leave this place empty. I glance at the cuff attached to my wrist. Crazy they left me here alone and I shot someone. Small town or not, my dad's friendship with the Chief or not, even I know this is a bootleg setup. I yell out one more time just in case.

I hear, thank God. "Give me a sec." The man's voice sounding like a beautiful symphony allows me to let out a sigh of relief. With each step he takes I can hear the keys jingling. I only see a silhouette of him as he approaches the door leading to me, he fumbles with the keys, the door opens and I stop breathing, because this man shouldn't be here. At all!

He doesn't look up to see has been yelling until he closes and locks the door behind him. Turning around, he stops and looks at me as if he Is looking at a ghost. "Merci, what in the hell?" I give him a smirk that I pray comes off as unwelcoming. I don't have the energy to panic or talk. I'm saving my words while also being cautious of what to say and what not to say. Knowing all to well the in front of me will strangle the life out of me.

My ex-boyfriend Brantley Dukes from Pratt, now walking over to me the limp still in his walk, that was caused by his actions towards me. "Not you Ms. Perfect." I say nothing I point towards the water dispenser. I need to stay in the moment. Brantley can have his verbally abusive way with me after I get what I need.

Surprisingly, he turns and looks to where my finger is pointing then he begins to walk over. I let out a silent sigh of relief. I close my eyes, this is becoming exhausting, tonight was supposed to be a celebration, a night that I cry tears of joy with my husband. I open my eyes feeling Brantley standing over me, looking up at him makes my stomach turn. I'm disgusted with myself. Was I that lonely to have been in s relationship with him? Yes, at that time I was extremely lonely.

He hands me the small cup of water. However, he places it in the hand with the wrist that has the cuff, just to be a dick. I grab the cup with my free hand, he starts taking, he gets some words out, I tune him out, because I want to enjoy this water Hydration is important, I should have put that into my thoughts before I turned myself in as well.

"What were you saying?" I ask breathing hard, also wanting more water. I crush the small paper cup in my hand, deciding to utilize it as a stress ball. "Genesis finally gets caught up and throws you under the bus." Brantley says leaning back on the front desk.

I have no idea what he is talking about. "The reason I'm here shouldn't concern you." Keeping a resting bitch face making sure to hold eye contact so he knows I'm not with his fake 'alpha-male bullshit. However, inside of me I'm nervous, this guy leaning on the desk is not a good person. His looks are deceiving. Brantley has aged well he is light-skin, squinted eyes, muscular build, sexy walk even with the limp, and big pretty white teeth hidden behind his thin lips. Brantley is very intelligent and in front of people he seems like the best person. At the beginning of us dating my dad believed Brantley was

Heaven sent. My dad and I would eventually find out he was sent straight from the pits of hell.

"I bet being cuffed to that chair is killing you right now?" he chuckles. I let the crushed paper cup fall to the floor. Being in the same building with him is the only thing killing me right now and annoying. "Baby, it's not like you going anywhere," Pointing at my wrist that is cuffed to the chair. He's right, I roll my eyes then let out a chuckle, "what's funny?" "Oh, nothing just thinking about the old days." I look at him with a sincere smile. "Yeah, what about those days?" he sounds interested in knowing. "That night Gabe slammed your head into the gravel at church camp." I lean my head back. "Also, Brantley don't ever call me baby again." I add catching the pattern of the ceiling, focusing the best I can, and drift back into the darkness.

I feel myself being restrained, but I only see darkness. "Merci, snap out of it. It's me Gabe I got you!"

CHAPTER 8

"Merci, it's me," I can hear Gabe, but I can't see him. "Let me go, let me go!" I hear a girl yelling and then realize that it's my voice. "Not until you calm down." His body presses against mine the more I try to break free. I start taking deep breaths, I learned this technique from the instructor at the anger management class that court ordered last year. I'm counting to ten, breathing in and out. Gabe begins to loosen his grip, but I pull him back in, he doesn't resist. He leans down and whispers in my ear, "you beat the shit out of that girl, good job!" His voice calms me, he knew that I needed to know that. Also, I don't know what happened after everything went black, so I'm glad to know I beat her ass. The smell of 'victory' is my favorite scent.

Still holding on to him I get on my tiptoes to whisper in his ear, "why didn't you kiss me?" He tenses slowly moving his arms from around me. "Merci, not here." He turns his head, I follow his gaze, I see a blurry Mike, my vision clearing up. Gabe saying, "not here", let's me know his brother really does not know what took place between us.

This makes me happy, because I know these twins tell each other everything, however for some reason Gabe made me an exception.

"Damn Merci, for a minute back there I thought you and Simone were twins, how ya'll cleared that table and beat them girls like they stole something." Mike high-fives me as he approaches us. "Wait!" Where is Simone?" I ask my anxiety peaking. "Calm down Quan has her outside in the front."

I get out of the front door, down the steps, and see Quan holding Simone in the road. She's an emotional fighter, seeing the tears didn't alarm me that she may be hurt, or she feels bad about a fight, her anger out in tears. "Simone!" I say loudly standing on the sidewalk. Quan releases her from their embrace, he doesn't look at me. Running up to me Simone is screaming, "Merci, we whooped them hoes!" she pulls me into a big hug, I squeeze her back. "Yeah, we did, and it was definitely worth the wait." I say back, Quan decides to look at me now and gives me a salute. I lift my middle finger up at him.

"Hey chick, I'm going to head home," I say releasing her from our long ass hug. She and I both look up at the benefit of living in a small town, the stars are always shining bright. "No, it's dark you can come with me, and Quan will drop you off, your daddy isn't home, we need to celebrate this shit. She looks back at Quan and he joins us on the sidewalk. "Merci, you've been wanting to beat that girl, and you did just that." As bad as I want to smile, I don't because I've never said I wanted to beat her to Quan, Mike, or Gabe. However, each of them has approached me with, "you finally got her" type words. I side-eye Simone and realize walking home is my best decision. Also, just because we beat those bitches up it doesn't erase that Quan fucked Kyomi earlier. I' mad for my best friend, but like always she's ignoring the real problem. The feeling of this being a 'setup' gone wrong is heavy in my spirit.

I'm sure I'll be okay call me later." I roll my eyes at Quan as I walk pass him, then begin the walk home. "I love you chick!" Simone yells behind me. "I love you too." I reply loud enough, without turning around.

I didn't' get far from where I had left Simone and Quan standing, when I hear Genesis yelling my name, as much as I want to stop I don't. My spirit is screaming for me to get home. "When the spirit is speaking, you obey." Is what my Grandma Eve always says. Genesis is still yelling my name as I'm turning down the sidewalk that will lead me to Simone's house, one more turn, then I cross the street and head up the hill that leads to my front gate.

I punch in the code. The gate slides open I walk through and hit the button for the gate to close behind me. I begin to replay every second of this evening in my head. Heading up the walkway, get to the front door, punch in that code I hear the door unlock, and I open the front door, slamming it behind me.

Falling to the floor the feeling of relief hits me. I'm home. I'm safe. I keep taking deep breaths to keep from passing out. Managing to sit up on my knees I close my eyes, tears start to flow down my face, then I silently pray. "God, I'm sorry for giving into my flesh, I'm thankful for the opportunity given to me this evening. I apologize for choosing violence, for I know you are a God of peace, I ask you for that peace right now. Thank you, God, and again I'm sorry, because they may not know better, but I do. In the name of wait God, I almost forgot, thank you for letting me finally have a few minutes alone with Genesis. That moment was amazing. Thank you, God in Jesus' name, Amen. Contrary to popular belief sincere prayers bring change you just have to believe.

I need to take a shower, the adrenaline is slowly leaving my body, I'm going to sleep good tonight, shit I deserve it. I'm standing up I look up at the staircase in front of me, hating I have to walk up the stairs to get to my bedroom. My body might not make it. Looking around at the house, it's dark, however the nightlights placed in different spots make it easy to see. I'm thankful to live in this house, however I do think a 6 bedroom and 5-bathroom house is a little much for a father and daughter. The garage is in renovation to become my dad's 'man cave'. He gave up his original 'man cave' to me as an entertainment room for my friends or when I have company over. I'm guessing he saw popularity in my future. No luck with that so far. The entertainment room has for all black 'Lazy Boy' relining chairs, a huge pullout sofa, a big screen TV, a refrigerator full of my favorite snacks, and a freezer is stocked with any flavor of ice cream you can think off.

Girls my age, who's fathers are friends or fellow pastors passing through, sometimes come over occasionally after church. Instead of the girls enjoying the room, they talk amongst themselves questioning how my dad can afford the material things we have. My dad says it's rude when I leave company downstairs, but he and I both know it's either I go to my room, or I beat them up. The students and faculty at my school refer to my house and the placement of it as the plantation on the hill. Insinuating my dad is the slave master, looking down from the hill to the slave quarters meaning the 'block'. If I sit and think about it, I can see understand the comparison. However, that's not the case, at least I don't believe it is.

I hit the light switch to the of me. I need more light to imagine that I am not home alone. Chances are good my dad will call sometime tomorrow evening to get all the details about what took place at the 'study session'. I will tell him everything, mostly justifying why it ended with me in a fight. He will understand, help me find the lesson in what happened, and then he will end the phone call with a prayer.

I make it to the top of the stairs thanking God. Looking left down the hall to where my dad's room is. I still can't believe that bitch asked me if my dad played a part in my mom's murder. What kind of outlandish question was that? Where would she pull that from? Out of all the questions she could've asked, why did she choose that one? My anger is rising at the thought of the question. My Grandma Eve says, "if you can replace a negative thought with a positive thought fast enough you can control your emotions. I think of how my dad still stares at pictures of my mom and the stories he tells me about her, he never refers to her in past-tense, as if she is still alive.

He's told me that when he and my mom moved here to Florida from Louisiana to start a new life. My dad found God shortly after getting here in Unity, he introduced God to my mom, started their own church, conceived me, and two years later she was shot and killed in front of the church.

Story goes from my grandma, my mom had been at the church after hours checking the books, whoever did it didn't take the money, the deposit bag was still in her hand. Our church is not too far from our house. I can see it from the front yard. My dad told me, my mom would always take her time, but that evening, something wasn't sitting right in his spirit. He decided to go check on her and found her laying not to far from the entrance of the church. That's all I know. Tynesha asking a question like that, not only threw me off, but it also hurt me as well. I literally gave her the best answer to her question.

I turn to the right, my side of the house, water is healing, and I need that right now. A familiar love hits me as I walk into my bedroom. Everything in our house is mainly white, furniture, white marble floors, the unnecessary pillars from the floors to the high-rise ceilings, the staircase, etc. The accent color to all of those things is black. Then there is my room, everything is my favorite color black.

My dad had a black headboard designed and built from some dude in Italy to make my canopy King Cali bed seem extra, the canopy sheets are a silky black color, the dressings of my bed, my carpet, my dressers, entertainment system, the outline of my mirrors, the curtains and blinds to my windows, my lamp shades, the inside of my shower, my towels, and the foot tub placed randomly beside the shower is in the color black. Basically, my bathroom floor, some of my clothes, and the light bulbs are the only things in my room that are not black.

I turn the knob in shower for the water to be extra hot, then stand in front of my bathroom mirror staring at my reflection due to the steam from the heat of the shower I disappear, letting the water do its job.

Feeling like I had been cleansed from the negative events that took place earlier. Stepping out of the shower, I dry my body off and tie it around me, grabbing a separate towel to dry my hair and exit my bathroom. As soon as I sit on my bed, the phone rings, I know it's Simone, but I don't have the energy to talk now. I only have energy to get this hair dry.

Wait! The thought pops in my head. Is the question Tynesha a real rumor that has been going around in this small town? I'm positive that Tynesha is not smart enough to come up with that by herself. I've never heard that, then again, I'm not around or out like that to hear rumors, The one rumor I have heard about my dad is his love for women, and I think that rumor is funny, because it's true. When the phone rings again I'll answer to ask Simone if she's heard that before, if she is lying, I'll be able to tell through the phone as if I am in her face. My hair is not completely dry, but no excess water is dripping. I need to get some homework done, the same homework I planned to do at the 'study session'.

Fuck! I left my bookbag at Genesis' house!

CHAPTER 9

"Girl! Why haven't you been answering the phone?" Simone must have been calling while I was in the shower, not just the one time after I got out of the shower. "I was just about to call you friend, I left my bookbag at Genesis' house, will you ask Quan to pick it up for me?"

The doorbell begins to sound off back-to-back. I roll my eyes knowing it must be Sister Hazel from the church, she's one of the few that have the code to the front gate. When my dad goes out of town, she in charge of checking on me. Sister Hazel could just call, however she wants the other women my dad has 'private session' to see her pull in without someone buzzing her in, so exaggerates by stepping out her car to enter the code. I guess she's his main chick if I were to put thought into it.

"Why doesn't she call," Simone asks the question that I am thinking. I can hear the irritation in her voice. Sister Hazel is rude all the time in and out of church. Simone's mom cussed her out two weeks ago at the grocery store, because Sister Hazel made it her point to let Simone's mom know her daughter is fast. Sister Hazel should have called tonight, because the way my mouth is set up from earlier. Now I'm going to have to explain to my dad a fight and cussing out an elder who is a devoted member to our church. "Merci, I have to tell you something,". Simone is saying as I hang up.

Leaving out of my room, speed walking to and down the stairs with the towel barely wrapped around me, barely holding up on my body, my hair is still hanging down my back air drying, I can feel the heaviness with every step probably will be an hour before it's fully dry, then I can put it in a bun before I go to bed.

The light I switched on, as I headed upstairs is the only light shining, however the porch light isn't on, and I can't see Sister Hazel standing on the other side of the door. Doesn't matter if I can see her or not, I'm opening the door and cussing her out. Taking a deep breath, I have a lot of things to get off my chest with 'nosey Sister Hazel'.

Swinging the front door, I step forward into the darkness on the front porch, because from the height of this person I have to gaze up. Slow motion sets in as I assess who I am looking at. Speaking is not an option, especially looking into his enchanting eyes, his eyes look as if they are glowing in the dark, noticing the dark brown speckles within the darkness of them.

"Merci." My name sounds as if he knows that I know that I belong to him. I need to play this cool though, it feels like my feet are stuck in cement, finally I manage to take a step back. I reach to my left hitting the switch that lights up our wrap around porch, the illumination causes us both to squint.

"Damn!" Genesis covers his mouth, having a slip of his thoughts spilling out his mouth again. Forgetting that I've come downstairs wrapped in a form fitting towel, he's staring me up and down. "You sure you see me everyday at school?" he asks crossing his arms across his chest, then taking a step back, to get a better look, at least that's what I think he is doing. "Yep, however you're always with her." I say refusing to say his girlfriend's name. Genesis steps back up closer to me looking down at me. "What if I wasn't with her?" his question is serious. My answer needs to be a good one. "You'd be here with me, and I doubt this towel would be around me." He puts his hands behind his head turning around as if he's contemplating whether to stay or walk away, but he turns back around.

"where's your Pops?" he asks, "he's out of town for the next week or so, why you want to come in?" Genesis is about tot answer, "Merci, here's your bag." Gabe says coming up the stairs, then it makes sense how Genesis got pass the front gate, the have the gate code and front door code. Once upon a time the twins and I hung out all the time and they would come spend time with my dad.

Gabe comes to an abrupt stop looking at me up and down, he knows what I look like with my clothes off, he knows what my skin feels like, and he knows what I taste like between my legs. I remember him being gentle, kissing me from my neck, sucking my breasts, working his way down kissing all over my stomach, and I wanted to know what his lips would feel like on my pussy, I showed no resistance. I hate that I am standing here getting wet off of memories.

I focus on Genesis and the reasoning for them being here to stop the thoughts of Gabe. "Genesis, man we have to go Quan just sent a 911 text." Genesis nods his head as if acknowledging Gabe and dismissing him at the same time. That's weird. Gabe hands me my bookbag. "See you tomorrow, Merci," Gabe says existing the porch. Getting on my tiptoes to watch him get in the passenger seat of Genesis' red BMW. "You and Gabe have something got something going on?" Genesis asks as I'm still looking at his car. How can he afford that car? Quan's BMW is blue, Gabe's BMW is white, and Mike's is black, but to my knowledge none of them have jobs. "Did you hear me?" his voice is demanding eye contact. If I answer 'yes' will Genesis be jealous or making sure he isn't pushing up on his friend's girl? "No, I'm checking out your car, my birthday is Friday, I'll be the big 16 and I'm wondering if my dad may have gotten me a car as nice as yours, but I won't know until he gets back in town." I feel crazy saying all that, because I don't know Genesis like that. "Genesis, Bro let's go," Gabe yells from the car.

"Cutie, your sweet sixteen is Friday? I know you coming to the party I'm having at my crib. I need you there, I want to celebrate with you!" Genesis is smiling and shrugging his shoulders moving to a song only he can hear, he's not hiding his excitement. It sucks, because I know what I'm about to say is going to disappoint and confuse him. I smile as I begin to back into the house. I'm getting in position to close the door, placing my bookbag in the house.

63

"I can't come to your party Friday, I know my dad isn't going to be home, however I spend my birthdays with my mom, see you tomorrow." I close the front door turning the lock, and I'm not looking back to see if he is standing there.

I think to call Simone, but hell by the time I get to my room exhaustion is present and potent. I unwrap the towel from around my bod, throw the extra pillows of my bed, pull my covers back, hop on my comfy King Cali bed, I don't remember falling asleep.

I jump up to my blaring alarm clock, reaching over to hit the button that will stop the noise. I see the time and I cringe, because I'm late for school. Taking in a deep breath, I say a prayer, "Lord whatever chaos this day may bring my way, turn it all into a beautiful symphony, in Jesus' name, Amen.

CHAPTER 10

I finish brushing my teeth and washing my face, admiring my naked body in the mirror, and blow myself a kiss. My Grandma Eve says, "you should never leave a mirror without encouraging yourself."

Rushing to my underwear drawer I throw on a red lace bra and matching panties, hit my closet up for some black cheerleading shorts, a black zip up sweatshirt and grab a pair of all black Adidas. I feel like this will be the day the janitor lady Ms. Blake is going to code me for the length of my shorts. If I leave now, I can make it to school by second period.

Running down the stairs I feel the soreness from the evening before, looking down at my hands, bruises are visible on my knuckles. I smile. Opening the front door, I come to a stop when I reach the last step to see Quan and Simone are sitting outside in his car. "What are ya'll doing here?". I ask breathing hard. "You weren't at school when the first bell rang, so I came to check on you," she explains. "Well let's go." Hurrying to the car. "Merci, where is your bookbag and those shorts are cute on you, but you already know Ms. Blake is going to give you detention." Simone is still talking as I enter the code to get back inside the house, run back upstairs to grab my bookbag, then turn back around as I remember I left my bookbag downstairs last night.

I'm breathing harder than the first time I made it outside. I hop in the backseat, thinking how I hate being late for school, it throws my day off. My 'bitch side' is in full affect, especially on an empty stomach. Thankfully, check on me and Quan tagged along even though I know he only came with her to be nosey. We arrive in the school parking lot in than two minutes, however I'm too late to catch the end of first period. Hearing Simone talking about what happened yesterday is getting on my nerves. When the car comes to a complete stop I hop out as fast as I can. My locker is where I need to be, because it is loaded with snacks and caffeinated drinks.

"Merci Genesis told me to tell you he put a note in the front pocket of your bag." Quan yells as I walk away from the car. I flip him off. Fuck Quan, Gabe, those sisters, Genesis, matter of fact fuck everything that took place yesterday evening and last night. That's how I'm feeling right now.

The first bell rings for second period, opening the doors leading to the main hallway. Everyday the hallway is usually loud and busy especially in between classes, not today at least when I enter, all eyes are on me. The realization that the only business that people will be minding today is mine.

Walking down the hallway random people are saying, "hey", well not random, but the the students speaking to me right now, weren't speaking to me yesterday. Kids don't want to be known for being friends with the pastor's daughter. Gabe and Mike are proof of that, most of our peers didn't know we were close friends until yesterday. So, the understanding I'm getting is the actions that took place yesterday makes it cool to be okay with me. That's weird.

To each, "What's up Merci", "Hey", or "Hey girl". I give a tight smile and a nod of my head. I won't be able to process any of this until I get to my locker that is holding all my goodies, trying to multi-task being nice and being hungry is something I am not good at. Finally, I reach my locker, our lockers are the color purple, instantly the color is annoying me, the lockers have always been purple, but because I am in a different head space my mind is finding small things to piss me off.

Getting my locker open I snatch the red can popping the top and begin to guzzle down the soda, if I were a vampire this drink is the equivalent of blood. "Hey chick, I've been searching for you all morning." Gabe says approaching me from behind. He waits for me to fini9sh drinking. When I feel satisfaction, I turn to give him my attention, "I woke up late." Again, trying to speak and catch my breath at the same time. Gabe isn't looking at my face, he's examining what I am wearing. "You want one?" reaching in my locker to hand him a soda. "Of course, I do." He answers licking his lips as I hand him the soda, but he hands it back. That's weird. "I must have heard you wrong when you asked what I want." Giving me a grin that assume is supposed to be sexy, however it's giving me 'whack' vibes. I'm hungry, no matter what he does my mind isn't going to register anything. I toss the unwanted soda can back in my locker, and reach for my jumbo honey bun, unwrapping it fast and go to work consuming it. In Gabe's eyes I may look like a mad woman how I'm devouring this honey bun, but I do not eat to be cute, I eat for sustenance.

Finishing the honey bun I toss the wrapper in my locker, grabbing a water bottle out taking only a few sips placing it back in the locker, then grab the book that I need for second period. I close my locker totally forgetting Gabe is still standing here. "What did you want again?" I ask, knowing it should have something to do with us running children's church tonight. At least that's the only time the twins and I communicate at school in front of other people and they both make those conversations quick.

"Merci, what happened between us over the summer meant something to me," Gabe says confusing me, because why is he bringing that situation up now? "Gabe, I wanted it to happen, you are the one that switched the vibe when we got home from camp." I see mike coming to join our conversation. "Merci". "Shut up, your brother is walking up." I whisper cutting him off. "Merci, or should I call you Mike Tyson? I'm proud of you." Mike gives me a high-five, he knows I'm not going to brag about violence, so I leave his hand hanging in the air. Picking up my bookbag, placing my book inside, while zipping up my bookbag I say to them both, "I'll see ya'll tonight, right? It's or turn for children's church, do not be late." I look up at them so they know I'm not with the stupidness or excuses they might try to come up with to not attend. "Yes, ma'am," the twins answer me in unison. "Merci," Mike says loudly before I can get too far down the hallway. I turn around rolling my eyes waiting to hear what he has to say. "You should wear your hair down more often, and Gen' told me to tell you he put a note in your bag somewhere." Gabe tenses at Genesis' name, I shrug my shoulders turning back around to head to class.

This whole time I have sent up prayers to God for Genesis just to pay attention to me, and he is, but I don't care. Waiting until last period of the day, I reach in the front pocket of my bookbag. Quan and Mike have continuously reminded me all freaking day about this note. I haven't seen Genesi, Tynesha, or Kyomi at school today. Cheerleading practice is canceled today and for that I am thankful. Today has been an outer body experience for me, students making small talk with me, Simone mentioned earlier that this is my first real day of popularity. I guess that whole 'pastor's daughter shit is out the window. "You are Merci now," she said earlier. Simone also thinks that it is a good idea to wear my hair down more often, but she's seen it down more than most and she's never made that suggestion before today. That's weird. Wearing it down everyday is not going to happen, checking myself in the bathroom earlier helped me decide once a week wouldn't be too much.

Opening the letter I get butterflies, it reads: "See you later.". They have been bugging me about a note that simply reads, "See you later,"? If Genesis believes that I'm ever coming back to his house, he is crazy. I fold the letter back neatly placing it back in the front pocket of my bookbag. Thinking about the way him and Tynesha kissed, even though she initiated to prove a point to me for some reason with her boyfriend, but he kissed her just as passionately, after we shared that moment on his porch. However, the situation that happened last night on my porch last night has me questioning somethings. Maybe we do need to talk.

This letter is going in to my 'high school memory box', and one day I'll go back through the box with my husband and laugh at how silly I was about my first crush. Soon this will all be a distant memory.

The bell rings. Simone is waiting outside of my classroom. "You okay chick?" "Yeah" I lie, because I'm not okay at all. This day has been twilight zone weird. I'm missing my dad. "Listen, I'm just going to head home since cheerleading practice is canceled.". Simone pulls me into a big hug, our hugs are always filled with love, however with the height difference between her and I the hugs can be awkward at times.

"I love you chick." She says as I back out of the hug. "I love you too." Getting choked up on my words, my period must be about to start, because I've been way too emotional.

On a positive note, to such a confusing day, I didn't receive a dress code violation for wearing the bare minimum of clothes. That is a massive, because I hate detention.".

PRESENT DAY: UNITY POLICE STATION 2004

"I know that you hear me!" Brantley is hovering over me. I don't have the energy to panic with him being so close to me. I am too fucking tired. "Nigga what?" my words are dragging, but I need him to desperately comprehend and feel my hatred for him. "I wasn't good enough for you, guess Genesis wasn't who you thought he was.". "Why do you keep saying that?", knowing this fool isn't getting what question I'm really asking. "Why do you keep using the word, was?". I ask in a way that he will understand. Brantley is intelligent, but he can be ditzy. My heart rate starts to speed up, damn I really didn't think this through, however it all happened so quick. I shot my soulmate in the chest without hesitation, it's sinking in now. That's weird. However, a life for a life.

"Merci, I haven't heard anything about your husband, that's why keep asking what' up with you being here cuffed to a chair." Brantley's voice holds assurance that he is telling the truth.

I waited 15 minutes after I shot Genesis to turn myself in and Mrs. Suthers is a member of our congregation, 1 of 3 people that work the front desk and dispatch didn't know either. I shot him in front of our congregation. By the time I opened the station doors she should have known. "Brantley, will you do me a favor. Check the front desk, check to see if any notes or anything pertaining to my husband is up there?" I make this request calmly. He takes a deep breath as if he wants to say 'no', however he's from a small town, so being nosey is in him. Watching him shuffling through papers from one end of the long desk to the other. He looks up at me. "Merci, there is nothing up here but this note. Holding it up, I squint, he should know from where he's standing, I can't read what's on the small piece of paper. He hurries towards me. The note has my name on it and under it in the same handwriting but written smaller it reads: "Don't believe her".

Looking from the paper to Brantley, I only feel confusion. While looking in his eyes and his eyes are silently saying the same thing. What the fuck is going on?

"Merci, something is wrong, did you speak with the Chief?". "No, he had to rush off to a wreck.". "What wreck?" Brantley asks. "You didn't hear it on your radio?". "No!", he is now pacing back and forth. He turns to look at me sympathy in his squinted eyes, walking towards me, I cringe as he leans down then unlocks the cuff. Rubbing the wrist that has been cuffed to get the blood circulating right, taking a deep breath and fall into Brantley's arms, tears start flowing from my eyes not letting up. Everything is hitting me all at once in this moment, I don't care if the sequins and rhinestones from dress my dress my be scratching Brantley up, but I'm dure he doesn't mind

He's speaking in a sweet whisper. It seems I'm always falling into someone's arms on a bad day. Closing my eyes then opening them, Brantley is sitting with me on the floor, holding me in the cradling position, realizing when I'm in distress or siting with a guy this position is always the position, I end up in. I look up at the ceiling letting the ceiling letting the tears flow out from the side of my eyes. I find a focus point on the ceiling. This day has been an outer body experience, I should be used to these kinds of experiences I've been having them for the last 10 years.

Brantley is holing me tightly. Brantley is giving me exactly what I need right now and that is a hug.

CHAPTER **11**

Walking home feels like I'm in one of those Spike Lee movies, just floating not feeling my feet hitting the ground. My feet finally hit the ground as I approach the front gate. Taking a deep breath, because the gate is open, Sister Hazel is probably waiting for me for her fake 'check-in' on me. I damn sure don't have time don't have the energy to cuss her out, I make a mental note to remind my dad she does not need a code to anything there is nothing wrong with her picking up the phone and calling.

Once I get up the hill not bothering to hit the button to close the gate behind me, I plan on her visit being short. I make it up the hill that gives a full view of our horseshoe driveway, but there is not a car in sight. With all rushing I did this morning. I may have forgotten to make sure the gate was closed. Mentally I will still fault Sister Hazel, she could have came earlier trying to figure out the code to the front door. It's possible. I get up the stairs, reaching then the front porch, and begin to press the numbers for the front door. "Do you always look angry when you come home from school?" He asks with humor in his voice.

I turn to the right, my eyes landing on Genesis. I need a hug and he may think what I am about to do is crazy, but I drop my bookbag, and run straight into his arms. Tears begin to flow down my face, he scoops me up and heads towards the front door. He's holding me in the cradle position, turning his head as I enter code for the front door. I hear him whisper, "this is crazy", I feel my body starts to go in a circle, he 's looking around the house. "Babygirl, you live here?". His question is rhetorical, so I say nothing.

"My room is upstairs to the right, it's the last door to the left," I say quietly through my tears. I guess yesterday evening and my day at school has really taking a toll on me emotionally. He kisses me on the forehead, his plush lips feel like I have always imagined. We get to my bedroom his actions of observing are the same as downstairs, finally he lays me on my bed. My tears are starting to ease up. "You feel like taking a nap with me for a few hours, before I have to go to church?" I ask sheepishly, knowing that kind of question may have caught him off guard. "Yes." He answers, he pulls of the black wife beater, keeping on his purple basketball shorts on. It's dark in my room, but with the little bit of light coming in from him not closing my bedroom behind him, I see his semi-hard dick print peaking through the thin material. I unzip my small jacket, "damn" I hear him whisper, looking down at my red lace bra, and remember that I didn't put on an undershirt, because of the rushing I did this morning.

I cross over to the right side of my bed, getting under the covers and he follow suit. We both adjust to each other's body while trying to get comfortable. My pussy throbbing feeling him along. I feel his hard dick pressing against my back of my right shoulder, while caressing my body, but not going under my shorts, just rubbing the outside. I know that he can feel my wetness through my shorts. "Let's try to go to sleep, I'm tired." I say in a low voice.

Not wanting things to go too far, because this situation is already wrong, because he has a girlfriend. I keep that in mind. Although, I know it's wrong I don't feel bad about it, but I refuse to give my virginity to someone that doesn't belong to me and then I end up just being a booty-call. Okay, cutie." He chuckles. "Do you really like living in this big ass house?" "It's just a house, material possession, it's not my home, home is where the heart is, and my dad is my home, so whether we live in this big ass house or a shack, as long as I'm with my dad, I'm home." I finish talking and snuggle in closer to Genesis' warm body, I feel the heaviness of my eyelids taking over. "I'm going to be your home one-day Merci." Genesis' voice says softly, I'm not sure if I'm supposed to say something back to him or if once again, he let his thoughts slip out of his mouth. "Wait, was the front gate open when you got here?" "No, I had to pay your boy Gabe to give me the code." So, I did remember to close it, even thought the gate was closed I'm still going to tell my dad that she does not deserve to have a code, because I don't need a babysitter.

"Hey, Merci, get up." Gabe's voice brings me out of my peaceful sleep as if he is my alarm clock. I sit up, nervously and star looking around the room for Genesis he's not in the bed anymore. My heart is beating hard, thinking I had just been caught in bed with a boy, Genesis or not it still would have been embarrassing. Falling back on my pillow and begin to look up at my ceiling. "Dude, I thought we were meeting at the church? Wondering if I had imagined Genesis even being here.

Leaning up to check the time. I don't attempt to cover myself up, because Gabe has seen me naked. "We still have thirty minutes before we have to be at church." Roling my eyes at him and snuggle back under the covers. Genesis' scent hits me, giving me confirmation that my mind hasn't been playing tricks on me, deeply inhaling his smell. It's intoxicating.

"I wanted to come talk to you, because I know we won't have time once we get to church." I peep from under the covers, because Gabe's voice sounds as if he might say something worth hearing. He walks towards my bed, gives me a nod as if asking for permission to sit. I nod back letting him know it's cool.

Truthfully, Gabe is sexy, he and Genesis are running a tight race in the sexy department. However, I watch how Gabe and Mike treat girls, they aren't mean just manipulators. Their light skin and good hair take them a long way. My grandma describes the twins as vampires. Nice to look at, enticing, but deadly. I believe their names are intriguing, Michael and Gabriel, makes them sound heavenly. Watching how they do those girls at school and church they way they do, that heavenly crap goes out the window. Hell, Gabe had me believing over the summer for a little while that we had something but turns out I was just another naïve girl.

I sit up leaning my back on my headboard, because no matter what did and didn't happen, I still consider the twins as close friends. So, if he feels we need to talk, I'll always be a listening ear. "What's up?" I ask. "Listen, I want to apologize about everything and hopefully you know what I mean when I say everything.", he reaches over to turn on the lamp on my nightstand, causing my eyes to squint my eyes from the brightness. When my eyes adjust to the light, I reply with a shrug of my shoulders. "Merci, you are special to me, I didn't tell my brother about the shit that went down between us over the summer, and you know I tell Mike everything.". A wave of relief hits me, knowing for a fact that Mike has no knowledge about our short-lived escapade. "Why are you apologizing now though?". I feel that my question is valid. Not waiting for his answer, I hop off my bed and head towards the bathroom to freshen up, also giving Gabe time to come up with his answer.

Pulling my hair into a bun makes me feel as if I'm zoning back into reality, it's not neat, because my hair has been down all day, however I'm satisfied. My thoughts go back to Genesis' arms around me and how good it felt to feel his hands touching my body. Looking in the mirror I smile and walk out the bathroom to throw on some clothes. Putting on a pair of black sweatpants laying on the floor over the shorts that I already have on, I grab a white tank top out of my dresser drawer, I go to my walk-in closet grab a black hoodie, and slide on my new all white pair of Adidas with black stripes on.

Gabe is standing up when I pick up my purse that I keep the keys to church in and head for my bedroom door. "Merci." He says, I turn to face him so I can look up in his eyes as he gives me the answer to my question. "I want to make things right, I've been digging you and I'm not going to lie, it didn't hit me how much until I saw Gen was trying to make a play." I love Gabe's honesty right now, but the audacity of this nigga! He wants to make things right with me, because someone else was trying to make a play on me. That' weird. "You are forgiven." is all I say walking out of the room, down the stairs, and out of the front door. I begin the short walk to the church. Gabe rides pass me in his car, as he should, because he knows what he just said was whack.

Children's church ran smoothly, the twins and I only have to teach once a month. The kids love when it's our turn to watch them, because they know we aren't going to teach a lesson. We allow the kids to do whatever they want as long as nothing gets broken, and the room is spotless before anyone can leave.

I choose to keep my distance from Gabe, but I could feel his eyes on me constantly for the two hours we were there. Sister Hazel popped in for a few minutes, apologizing for not checking in on me last night. She didn't mention anything about a fight, which was surprising, I assumed that news would have circled around our small town 20 times over by now. She did inform me that my dad would be calling me later tonight, that information made my heart smile. I have never seen Sister Hazel seem so chipper, she's a red-bone, butterball shape, attitude wise she is either hot or cold, but she was luke warm talking to me. That's weird.

CHAPTER 12

My phone is ringing as soon as I step in my bedroom, I know it's Simone. I tell her about the whole Genesis and Gabe situation that happened after school, she is unusually quiet listening. "What's wrong?" I ask, knowing if she is quiet something isn't right Simone confesses that Quan had told her once Gabe has a 'thing' for me. Instead of being mad at her I feel bad she has had to keep that information from me, but I haven't told her the whole Gabe story, so I guess that makes us even.

"Simone, do you believe that Tynesha and Genesis are done?" I want to know what my best friend's honest opinion, because these are her people, and she knows how they operate. Also, I'm not trying to be a side piece. "Merci, I wouldn't read too much into Genesis, I'm not going to lie, I've never heard or seen him doing no shit he did with you last night or today, but." she stops talking, "but what?" I ask preparing myself for what she is about to tell me. "Quan had to stop by Genesis' earlier, I didn't get out, but Tynesha's car was there." She spills the information, and I don't have a response. Tears forming in my eyes.

"Sorry friend, that bitch must have some kind of spell on him." While Simone is in the middle of talking, I hang up the phone.

A few tears fall from my eyes, I hear my Grandma Eve's voice in my head, "men blow like the wind, can't make up their minds on which direction they want to blow." I walk over to my window, pull back the shades back, and open the blinds. Looking down at the beautiful waterfall my dad had built after my mom died. I want to ask her for advice. I bet she wouldn't have fell for Genesis' mind games.

My dad encourages me to talk to my mom when I go spend time by the waterfall, he says just because I can't see her or hear her, but she is always listening. I watch the water change to emerald green he had lights installed to give the illusion the water changes to that color. The next color is aqua blue those were her favorite colors. I go talk to her on Sundays after praise and worship service I rarely stay at church long enough to hear my dad preach I enjoy the music and that's how I like to show my appreciation to God by clapping, singing, and dancing. I also go talk to her if I am feeling overwhelmed. Maybe, I should call my grandma, she gives the best advice. I hate watching her grow old, eventually she'll be gone too, but hopefully no time soon. Being a teenage girl without a mom sucks. Taking a deep breath to calm down, the phone rings, rolling my eyes, backing away from my window.

"Hello", I answer with an attitude. "My Babygirl! What's going on?" My dad's voice is everything, he really is my home. I hop on my bed making sure not to tangle the phone cord as I lay on my back. "It's a lot daddy." "Then get to talking and leave nothing out, I'm all ears." Giving my dad the whole run down leaving nothing out, if I were to leave anything out, then there would be holes in my story, also I don't like lying to my dad.

When I finish, he bursts out in laughter, causing me to have to pull my ear away from the receiver, because he has a hearty and loud laugh, that he will be remembered by. I envision his wavy low-cut hair with the grey streak placed perfectly on the left side of his hairline, his wide smile and huge wolf like teeth sparkling. He stands a good 6'7, with dark chestnut skin and he makes sure to stay in the gym. I miss him even though he is on the phone right now. His voice is deep, mesmerizing, and powerful. The louder he speaks the more you can feel his power.

His laughter comes to an end. "Merci", he says my name in a serious tone causing his Louisiana accent to come out a bit. "Do you know why your mother and I gave you the name Merci?" he doesn't give me time to answer. "God is merciful you are not, I understand all of that teenage stuff, you were supposed to beat that heifer, but that Genesis boy, I don't like, however I do appreciate and his mother in many ways for being a faithful member of our congregation. One day he's going to get Gabriela and Michael in trouble, I'm still trying to figure out how those boys came across those cars." I stay silent knowing my dad isn't done speaking.

"Babygirl, you have a good head on your shoulders, stay focused and keep your guard up. Take advantage of your new popularity status, also think about Gabriel being more than just a friend, because if I had to choose for you, it wouldn't be Genesis." He finishes. "Daddy, I'm going to feel stupid seeing Genesis at school with his girlfriend tomorrow." I confess. "Girl put your poker face on until you get home, hell do something to shake his world up." My dad's voice sounds cold. "I'm sure I can do that."

I know exactly what I am going to do, it's risky, however it will get the job done. "That's my girl, now say your prayers, let God lead you, also you can miss school Friday, you can't deal with this foolishness on your birthday, so make it through tomorrow and then enjoy your three-day weekend. I'll call you Friday on your birthday, I love you baby girl, but don't have Genesis in my house again, goodnight." He hangs up before I could say 'I love you too'.

I say my prayers. My eyelids grow heavy as I think about all the possibilities of what is going to come out of my plan. Tomorrow should be anything less than interesting. It's not just Genesis that needs to learn a lesson, Gabe needs to be taught a lesson as well. God forgive them both for they know not what they have done by playing with my feelings.

CHAPTER 13

"You've been all smiles since we left your house." Simone says. I love walking to school with her, however it's weird, because she has to walk pass the school to get to my house. As we cross the street and approach the school, the butterflies start to form in my stomach. The sky is beautiful, the sun shining bright is adding to my excitement. Everything seems to have techno-color look right now. I believe making someone jealous is a great way to serve payback. Genesis is an asshole for his actions and Gabe keeping secrets about his feelings is whack. So, I have decided that I will kill two birds with one stone, however one of the birds will be brought back to life with a kiss, he will never forget. They both like to act off confusion, therefore confusion is what I will give them. Looking over at Simone, "I have a feeling today is going to be a great day".

I'm glad Simone told me about seeing Tynesha's car at Genesis' house, if she hadn't, I would be coming to school with a different mindset. Straight blind-sided if I were to see them together after he was in my bed, now that's something that may have sent me into breakdown mode. I love Simone for her honesty whether it's going to hurt my feelings, she is going to keep it real with, I'm blessed to have her as a best friend. She always has my back in every situation, and I reciprocate her actions, love, and honesty without question.

Today she will feel out of the loop, however I'll explain to her later why I had to keep this plan to myself. Walking through the parking lot, like yesterday people are speaking to me, I have never heard my real name spoken this much at school, elementary school, my name has always been 'Pastor's daughter', or something related to church. I'm grateful for the change.

Simone's purse drops, everything spills out. I bend down to help collect her things. Her purse has everything, but the kitchen sink inside of it. We get her things back in the purse, I stand up brushing the gravel off my jeans. "Look at that shit." I follow Simone's hate-filled gaze and see the 'shit' she is speaking on.

Genesis is walking in the double doors of the gym, holding hands with his girlfriend. I decide to say nothing, but this nigga has lost his mind. My dad's voice pops into my head, "your name is Merci, nut that does not mean that you have to give or show Mercy." I wonder how cutthroat my dad once was, because most of the advice he gives me goes against what's in the Bible. My grandma says my mom was a 'beast', my parents may have created a hybrid. Me. That would explain my temper and my belief that violence is the answer to most situations. I need to focus.

"Don't let them ruin your day chick, he tried to trick you, at least you know what's up and you didn't let things go too far." She says heading to the doors that lead to the main hallway. Thing is Genesis didn't trick me, because I didn't ask him if he and her were over.

I reconsider my plan, then my flesh overtakes my spirit full force. I've always heard that Genesis is the faithful type, he may flirt, but that's as far as it goes. From the outside looking in I chose to believe that until yesterday when he was waiting for me to get home, how he easily he got bed with me, making himself comfortable, caressing my body, and his words, "I'll be your home one day." I should have asked him.

I've prayed for Genesis to somehow be in my life, proving that I need to be careful what I pray for and be more specific because I got who I wanted. However, I didn't know all this other bullshit would come with it. Real deal my heart is breaking.

The bell rings ending 4th period, it's 'go' time. Simone and I have the same lunch as Genesis and his crew. Simone and I usually sit inside the cafeteria, to spend one on one time. I call it 'catching up with Simone time', because she tells me all the gossip, she's acquired so far during the first four periods of school. Today I decide we should sit outside. We get our food. She heads towards the table we picked our freshman year as ours. "Simone, we should sit outside, it's beautiful outside." I suggest with a smile. She gives me a one shoulder shrug and follows me to the side doors of the cafeteria that leads to the lunch patio where the 'popular' people eat lunch. I don't turn around to see the expression on Simone's face, I don't need her asking about my sudden need to eat outside. I'm on a mission. Finding the perfect spot for us to sit was easy, we sit at the table in perfect view for everyone sitting with Genesis can see us. Sitting down Simone is unusually quiet, I look at her and I think this is the first time that I have seen her uncomfortable. I look up to see Genesis looking at me 'confusion' looks good on him. He probably didn't know that we share the same lunch time. Genesis moves closer to Tynesha, whose face looks like she was in a fight and didn't win. I give him a big grin and wave at him. Homeboy is rude and doesn't wave back, instead he licks his lips, gives me a wicked grin, puts his arm around his girlfriend pulls her in, and gives her a kiss on the cheek. That's cute. I assume this is his way of telling me, she is where he wants to be, however my poker face will not fall.

The guy that I want in this moment is walking up to our table right on time. He is apart of my plan and doesn't even know it. I get up from the table fast, to pull this off correctly and effectively. I walk up to him. "Merci, everything okay you always sit inside, I was coming to check on you?" I don't answer Gabe's question, I get on my tiptoes and press my lips against his. Gabe draws back, then he goes in lifting me up to his level rubbing my back and squeezing my ass. "You better get it girl!" I can vaguely hear Simone saying loudly in the background. She's loud enough to catch everyone's attention. Yes, this kiss is to make Genesis jealous, but this kiss is also to let Gabe know that I am interested in him too. I'm still in my feelings about the reason he decided to finally confess his feelings for me, but this kiss is real. It's my first kiss and I'm sharing it with someone who cares about me for real.

My head is spinning once the kiss ends, I smile up at Gabe, then attempt to wipe my red lip gloss off his lips. However, he grabs my hand and gives it a kiss, letting me know that he doesn't care the lip gloss is there. We speak no words. Our eyes speak for us. I turn back heading to the table I left Simone sitting. Gabe goes back to his crew. I watch them all dapping it up and giving each other high-fives, everyone except Genesis. Simone looks from their table, then back at me, "well that was entertaining and unexpected." Covering her smile to hide her smile. Genesis his dark eyes are piercing through me, I feel his anger. I give him a wink. He turns his head away from my direction, I watch him give Gabe a dap, but his face holds no expression.

I look at Simone, "you're welcome," I say sticking my tongue at her, and we both burst out in laughter.

PRESENT DAY: UNITY POLICE STATION 2004

"Merci, wake up we have to figure out what's going on." Brantley is saying with urgency in his voice. "I am awake, I was just thinking with my eyes closed." I say sitting up, removing myself from his hold. I sit on the floor beside him. "Don't believe her? What is that supposed to mean?", "I don't know dude, everything seems to either be a secret or plans I make alone, or plans made without me that I'm never supposed to find out about, it could mean anything." I'm talking out loud, Brantley may think I'm talking to him, but I'm talking to myself.

"Did you plan to shoot Genesis?" Brantley's question is valid and a good question. "Of course not, but tonight I found out the truth." "What's the truth"? he asks. I look over at Brantley, I stand up, walk over to the water dispenser, fill the small paper cup with water chug it down, then walk back over to the sit I have been sitting in since I turned myself in. "Will you come and put the cuff back around my wrist?" I ask Brantley politely. "Why?" he asks. I just remembered you can't be trusted, and I feel something isn't right, because you shouldn't be here." I say as honestly as I can, without an attitude.

"I see you are still the same bitch from back in the day." He is mad, putting the cuff around my wrist tighter than the first officer had before. "There's the Brantley I know, I had begun to think you had changed, however once a nutcase always a nutcase." Giving him a lop-sided smirk. He backs up, "fuck you bitch." He means those words. My reply is a nod with my head. Brantley has always been jealous of Genesis. Jealousy of another man being with someone they want, especially if that guy blew his chance, will drive that man crazy. Well, Genesis made Brantley go fucking crazy,

He heads towards the back where he had come. I look up at the ceiling find a pattern and fall back into my thoughts.

88

CHAPTER 14

Jealousy is one of the deadly sins, and if you make it a point to open Pandora's box labeled Jealousy inside of a person you can't close it. You can make a choice. However, the consequences are not yours to choose. Genesis made two choices yesterday: One, to come paly in my bed. Two: after he left my bed he went home to be with his girlfriend. Consequently, I chose to respond to his choices with a kiss. A kiss to make him jealous and assure Gabe that my feelings for him match the feelings he has for me. Unfortunately, I had to show Genesis that I don't play checkers, my dad taught me to play chess at a young age.

After lunch, the rest of the school day flashed by. Gabe surprises me as I walk out of my last class, standing outside of the door. I don't hide my smile. Is this what it feels like to have a boyfriend? Technically, Gabe and I aren't an official couple yet, at least I don't think so. He takes my bookbag off my shoulder then grabs my hand. Right now, it's looking as if that's the route we are taking. All eyes are on Gabe and me from the hallway, all the way to the parking lot to his assigned parking spot. The whole crew is posting up at their cars.

Simone and Quan are both looking at us smiling and nodding as if giving their approval.

"Thank God, now we don't have to share anymore, love you, Merci! Mike says, saluting his brother. His words make me smile, because that may have been another reason Gabe chose not to pursue me, he didn't want to share with his brother. I wouldn't have let that happen anyway. "I see you boy." Genesis comments as we walk pass his car, Tynesha is sitting in the passenger seat. "You better." Gabe's response is dry and direct. That's weird. He doesn't make eye contact with Genesis. His grip tightens on my hand. I walk closer to him and use my free hand to caress his arm for reassurance, that I'm with him.

The kiss I shred with this light skin heartthrob threw me off, if I'm honest being honest with myself. I want more, not sex more, but the safety in knowing Gabe really does care about me. He's always made me feel safe. I'm glad Genesis did what he did after he left me yesterday

We get to Gabe's car. He heads to the passenger side to open the door for me. The gesture is cute. However, I walk home for reason. I use the short walk to clear my mind and release the bad energy. I scrunch up my face, because I feel Gabe isn't going to like my next move. I hold my hand out for my book bag, he rolls his eyes, while handing me my bag, for the second time today I get on my tip toes, nuzzling my nose against his. Gabe links is arms around me, and a kiss happens again, but it's more passionate than the first. His dick is growing, I can feel it poking me through his thin gym shorts. I pull away moving my lips from his mouth to his ear. "Later, I promise." Giving him a quick kiss on the cheek, then begin my short walk home.

I wonder if I am going to be a good girlfriend, still unsure if I am Gabe's girlfriend. Why did Gabe respond to Genesis' congrats like that? Is Mike honestly okay with his brother and I being together? Thankful that they canceled cheerleading practice again today, I finally have time to think and process everything. My 16th birthday is tomorrow, but since that fake 'study session' on Tuesday, I haven't had time to be excited about my age milestone. I'm definitely glad I get to stay home from school tomorrow, but from the week this week has been going, I know some bullshit is going to transpire. Things are calm right now, but when things, and people are calm that's when you know a storm is coming. And it doesn't help that it's a full moon tonight.

I want to escape in a book even if only for a few hours, reading is my favorite past-time. I get home fix, then head upstairs already deciding that my book of choice is 'Their Eyes Watching God' by Zora Neale Hurston the excitement of getting caught up in words starts to build. The doorbell sounds off, I roll my eyes, damn the devil is busy. I've made it midway up the stairs with my snacks, now I have to turn around go back down these stairs and open the front door, and I have no idea is behind it. What I do know is, this week every time I've opened the front door there is always a weird situation on the other side.

Opening the front door, no one is in front of me. I hear a vehicle and see the tail end of a van with flowers painted on the back, leaving out of the driveway. I look down there sits a vase full of black roses, I don't have to count the roses. I've received a vase of a dozen black roses since I can remember on my birthday. The flowers are beautiful, but the vases they are placed in get more extravagant every year. No card is attached as usual, my dad swears he knows nothing about where these roses come from who. My Grandma Eve honestly does look confused if she is visiting during my birthday and sees the roses. The roses also make her angry, it makes her think that I have a stalker, she also gets worried, because the person or people who killed my mom were never found.

My dad never seems worried. "Maybe they are from your mama," the times when he says that I stay silent, I can't call him a liar, that would be disrespectful. I have placed my snacks by the little table by the door to free up my hands and pick up the vase. This one has my name engraved on the side as I set the table. Supposedly, my mom and I share a lot in common, our handwriting included, if I took a quick it does look like my handwriting, but the 'M' is slanted. I stare at the name on the vase. The "M" is in the handwriting of how my mom wrote in my baby book. I star thinking the impossible, what if my mom is alive? If that is the case, I'm punching her in the face. However, I believe it's my dad that sends the roses. Giving the vase one more glance before I head upstairs, I wonder why the delivery is a day early. I pick my snacks up and head back upstairs.

Two hours into my reading the phone rings, I answer, "Hello." "Merci!" I slam the receiver down ending the call. Genesis' voice caught me off guard, but I do not want to hear anything from him. The nerve of that dude. Returning to my reading, losing myself in the words, the phone rings, Simone gives me no time to say "Hello". "Merci!", "what's wrong?". "Girl, get to my house now." She hangs up. It doesn't matter what is going on anyway, because she knows that I'm coming. Thankfully, all I have to do is put on my shoes. Rushing out of my room, down the stairs, ad out the front door.

Simone is waiting for me at the end of her sidewalk that leads to her house, she doesn't look mad. The way she is standing, knowing her body language she is annoyed by something. "Dumb ass niggas." Are her words as I stand beside her. "You, okay?" my breathing is shaky from running to get to her. She gives me a nod assuring she is. I look at what has her attention, Gabe and Genesis are standing face to face. "What's going on?" I ask out loud, however the question is for me. I look up at Simone, "What am I supposed to do?" she grabs my hand and leads me towards the chaos. "You have to choose one, Merci." Simone should already know who I'm going to choose. This will be quick.

CHAPTER 15

"**D**amn, Merci you already staring shit in the group." Quan is laughing, he is happy that none of this has to do with him. All I see is Genesis and Gabe are having a close body staring contest, or that's what I see. I peep Mike standing caddy corner across from Genesis, if Genesis swings Mike is in the perfect position to knock him out. Mike catches me looking at him, his eyes relay that he is not my friend right now.

This situation is my consequence of the choice I made at school to use Gabe, although I do have feelings for him, I made a decision to involve him to make another person jealous based off temporary emotions. To assure my feelings for one boy, but at the same time hurting another, so this is my consequence.

"You knew though nigga!" Genesis' tone is aggressive. "Get out of here with that shit I didn't know anything." Gabe's voice holds the same aggression if not more. Oh shit! "Matter fact Gen I been could have had that, you don't even know what she tastes like." Gabe says causing my jaw to drop. Why would he say that? "Simone did he really just say that?" I ask to be sure I heard Gabe right. "Yes, you want to jump him?" Simone looks back at me. Genesis is looking at me over Gabe's shoulder, his eyes aren't dark I can see the light brown speckles shining in his eyes. It's time for me to step in.

"Yeah, you ate my pussy over the summer, big freaking deal." I speak loud enough so everyone can hear. "We didn't have anything else to do." I add, Simone nudges me as if I need to shut up. I shrug my shoulders. "Gen is being greedy." Mike speaks for his brother." This shit is whack, Merci pick who you are going to let hit, we need to get back to business." Quan says squeezing in between Gabe and Genesis, placing a hand on each of their shoulders.

I start to back away, looking at their crew, and begin to understand this not the first or last time they'll deal with a situation like this when it comes to females, I'm just the pick of the week. "So, I get to choose?" I ask with excitement in my voice, placing my hands over my mouth as if I've just been called down like the white people when they get called down on 'The Price is Right' to add to my dramatics. Simone giggles, because she knows as much as I do these niggas got me fucked up. "Well Cedrick, if I must make a decision, I choose me, fuck ya'll."

I turn to head home, "Simone, call me tomorrow." I know she'll be at my house before she goes to school in the morning, because it's my birthday. I left a good book for this shit. However, I can't lie it feels good to have two fine ass dudes squaring off over me. I smile the whole way home.

"Hello?", "Hey baby!" My Grandma's Eve voice wakes me up Her voice is warm. "Tell me what las given you?" she asks. Loving how she holds to speaking how she wants. The older she gets the more her words get twisted or come out like riddles. I begin telling her everything even the intimate details. I know by the end of our conversation she will tell me exactly what I need to hear.

"You are your mother's daughter. She resides heavily inside of you." Are her words when I finish giving her the rundown. "How so grandma?" "Your mama had two handsome and powerful young men pursuing her when she was around your age, she had the hardest time choosing between the two. The men had a close bond, a bond no woman should ever find herself tangled in. Eventually, she made a decision, but she didn't make it easy for either one of them. I told your mama to never compromise her heart, because if you love yourself, your heart will help you choose. If a man tries to force you to choose that's not love, now I'll tell you the same. Merci, be mindful, you will know and keep in mind a man can always be replaced, however a broken heart cannot."

Grandma is still talking as I grab the phone and pull the cord to my window, lifting the blinds up to get a view of the waterfall. I'm glad my mom's heart chose my dad, also knowing he had to put in work for her heart, makes me smile and their love story more romantic. "Anywho, I wanted to call and tell my one and only grandchild happy birthday, I know that I am a day early, but I'll be boarding a cruise ship in the morning, and I won't be able to call you, so again happy birthday and always choose you baby girl. I'm proud of you and I'm pretty sure wherever you mama is she is proud of you too." "I love my grandma still dates and lives her life I pray I will be like that in my older ages. "Thank you, grandma." "I love you Merci, more than you will ever know, happy birthday now go to bed."

She hangs up, but I still have the receiver of the phone in my hand. Tomorrow night at 6pm I will be wearing my all-new black lace dress, let my hair hang, decorate the bench with the 12 black roses, put the three chocolate cupcakes that my dad will have delivered in the morning, place a candle in my cupcake, light it, and make a wish. This is going to be my first birthday without my daddy, and the 14th without my mom. She was shot two months after my 2nd birthday. I'll be alone, but no need to break tradition.

Hanging up the phone, I hop on my bed and say my prayers. If it's the Lord's will, when I wake up, I'll be 16 and still a virgin. In Unity that's an achievement.

"Brantley?" he answers me by raising his eyebrows, "what do you want now?" he's asking me as if I've been bugging him. He's only gotten that one small cup of water for me once.

"Do you remember those two sisters Tynesha and Kyomi, I heard they transferred over to Pratt, after Christmas break, so the beginning of '95 the second semester of our sophomore year?" "Hell yeah, those girls were the best thing to happen to us at Pratt." I see he is reminiscing about the old days. I won't even imagine the fuckery that may have taken place with them and those sisters, he never mentioned them when he and I were dating.

"Did either of them ever say why they left Unity?" Brantley hops off the side of the front desk that he has been sitting on, walking towards me, at least that's how it looks. Thankfully, he sits in the chair next to mine. He's still to close for my comfort. "I never asked, didn't care, but there was a rumor that one of them were pregnant." He pauses for a second, "which ever one that was supposedly pregnant, the baby daddy was from Unity." I sense that's all of the information he has about those hoes. "Interesting." I say nodding my head,

Brantley continues to sit beside me silently. I remember the last time I saw the sisters at Unity High, my eyes were filled with tears, and my heart was being torn out of my chest, but I saw them.

I have no need to focus on the ceiling to travel back to my memories. Especially, the day of my 16th birthday and the events that took place afterwards. I learned quickly what Betty Wright meant in her song with her words, "a little bit of pleasure is worth a whole lot of pain."

CHAPTER 16

"Happ birthday best friend!" Simone is screaming, days like this I wish she didn't have the code to the front door. I have been peacefully. At least she's not jumping up and down on my bed. I yawn, sit up stretching my arms out, to look up at her and quickly lay back down pulling my covers over my head.

"Simone why in the hell are all ya'll in my room?" I ask, the real question is why they are all soaking wet. Simone didn't come to wish me happy birthday by herself. I saw she has Quan, Mike, and Gabe standing behind her. "Simone! I want them out!" I yell out from under my covers, I know I'm being a bitch, but it's my birthday and I can be a bitch if I want to. I knew for a fact that she would come by before and after school on my birthday. She also knows she is the only person outside of my dad that I want to see on my birthday. "Girl why are you tripping?" that can't be a real question. Giving a low growl from under the covers as my answer. Lifting the covers from the side to see what time it is. 7:10am, this isn't real, I can no longer control my anger.

Throwing the covers back, sitting up fast, I want her to see the anger on my face, while hearing it in my voice as well. The company that she brought with her, have exited. "Are you being serious right now, you show up with these assholes like yesterday didn't happen, with that being said Gabe is the last person that I want to see." My attitude is potent in my voice. Simone opens her mouth to speak, but I cut her off, by holding my hand, because I am not done talking. "Look, I know you enjoy and entertain the stupid shit, and that's cool however I'm not trying to play games like you and Quan." I realize I'm taking my anger out on my best friend, however I don't feel bad for any of the words coming out of my mouth. Out of all people Simone should know better. I lay back down, looking at the ceiling.

"Bitch what? It's your birthday, I'm here as I always am. When Quan came to pick me up, the twins were already in the car." Now she is mad. "Happy birthday, Merci. By the way school is canceled today, because of that bad storm that hit last night, just in case your grouchy ass is wondering why we are wet. We got soaked trying to find you some flowers or something, but all the stores are out of power, we've been running around in the rain for you." I lift up in time to see her walking towards my bedroom door. With her back to me as if she can feel me looking at her, she says, "glad it took me trying to put a smile on your face, to find out how you really feel about my relationship." Simone slams the door. The electricity is out I look over at my alarm clock and remember its powered by batteries.

Tears are forming in my eyes, I feel bad for unleashing my anger on her, but I meant every word. She should've at least made them wait outside, especially Gabe. I must have been sleeping hard, because I can hear the rain falling hard on the roof, the thunder is booming, and I bet when I look outside the lightening will streaking across the sky. I begin to pray, "Please Lord, my birthday is starting off with chaos, show me grace and let it end with a beautiful symphony in Jesus' name, Amen.

I hop off my bed and head over to my window, I can't see through the rain, but just as I thought the sky is lighting up with lightening strikes. Having nothing to do I head back to hop on my bed to think of ways to apologize to Simone, while making it clear, I'm apologizing for how I said it not for what I said.

I hear laughter coming from the other side of my door, because with the electricity being out the laughter sounds clear and closer it's echoing. I hop off my bed with a smile, navigating through the extra darkness in my room for clothes to put on and go join my company who have decided to stay after being dismissed.

Locating the hoodie and sweatpants I wore last night to children's church. Heading out of my bedroom, I remember to grab my toothbrush, toothpaste, facial wash, and a towel to freshen up. I carefully exit my room, taking in the light, and thankful that outside of my room everything is white and open, it's still dark because of the storm but I can see, the electricity is not needed out here.

I get to the kitchen pantry, grabbing one of the gallon jugs of water that we have for times such as these. I freshen up at the kitchen sink. As I am wiping my face. I hear Simone. "Gabe, when Merci gets in here ya'll are going to tell us this mysterious camp story." I shake my head contemplating whether I should go back upstairs. "Yeah, I with

Simone, you didn't tell me nothing, and the crazy thing is I was t camp with ya'll, I guess I was distracted." I smile hearing Mike speak about not being in the know of what had taken place. "We are just being nosey" Quan blurts out, I respect his honesty. "Stop!" Gabe says loudly, I'm listening from the kitchen, but I want to see his face. "I didn't tell anybody, because I messed up when we got back home trying to impress ya'll niggas." He explains.

"Yeah, he definitely messed it up." I say entering the room, heading straight for the refrigerator, hoping the drinks inside are still cold, because I'm not sure how long the electricity has been out, grabbing my soda, and thanking God I leave lip gloss randomly around the house. Turning around to face everyone, I see they have all made themselves at home. Simone is sitting on Quan's lap in one of the reclining chairs, Mike has found his way back to his old spot, at least he remembers. I smirk him, because the look on his face shows he misses this room. Gabe is standing by the window, since I'm in a guessing mood, I guess he's been waiting on me before he takes a seat. Making eye contact with me I give him nothing, then take my usual seat.

"Nope, we are not about to act like this summer shit isn't something we don't need to know about, because yesterday was crazy and could have been avoided if we knew ya'll had something going on, we boys and it went too far." Mike is right in a way, but what does knowing the whole story have to do with anything. Also, using friendship as a reason to know about a situation, that two people kept to themselves is whack. The room is quiet, I take this moment of silence to apply my lip gloss, pop open my soda, take a few sips allowing the caffeine to do its job.

Truth is Mike and Gabe left me behind, we are two grade levels apart, however when I entered high school, they never welcomed me with open arms. I believed the twins would have at least help me navigate my first day or two. That didn't happen. Before their freshman year we would hangout all the time, they came over here everyday

My feelings were hurt for a while, then I spoke to my dad about it, he reminded me with age comes change, and the twins had changed. "Mike you and Gabe left me, you both know that I have no family, you two were my family, but when ya'll hit high school it's as if I didn't exist to ya'll anymore." I finish speaking my truth. Simone and Quan begin to laugh, making it seem as if my hurt about the twins abandoning me humorous. The twins join their laughter. "Oh, ya'll think it's funny, ya'll can leave, but for real this time." And I mean they can leave, because there is no reason to laughing. I catch Gabe giving Mike a smile and a nod.

"Damn, Merci calm down, we are not laughing at you, because you don't pay attention to shit, especially at school. "Quan stops talking looks at Simone, as if asking for permission to keep talking. "What?" I'm confused, because I do pay attention, however only to who and what I feel deserves my attention. I look at Quan wanting to know what I've been missing when it comes to the twins. "My boys are too busy jacking dudes up protecting you from dudes that just look at you the wrong way, that's what you haven't been missing, get out of your head." It makes sense what Quan is saying, because it's been numerous occasions a dude spends all day flirting with me then the next day that same dude will walk by me as if the day before didn't happen. "Boy whatever." I respond by rolling my eyes.

"It's true what Quan is telling you is the truth." Gabe is saying coming towards my chair, lifting me up and placing me across his lap with my legs hanging off the side. "Ya'll see how smooth my brother just did that?" Mike asks laughing, but not wanting an answer. Simone looks at me with a smile nodding in approval. Quan looks over at Gabe and cocks his head to the side, "you two do might make a cute couple." Simone slaps him on the shoulder. "Merci, why have I never been in your house?" Quan asks. Not taking my eyes away from Gabe's who is still apologizing silently while squeezing my left thigh tightly and rubbing my lower back lightly. "I don't like you Quan." We all can't help but to laugh at my brutally honest answer.

"Okay, now that we have this part straightened out, and you understand that we weren't ignoring you but protecting you, can we please have the story?" Mike is desperate at this point to know what went on. "I'm going to be honest I think Gen should be here for this so he can have some clarity on the situation." Mike adds. "That nigga doesn't need to know everything." Gabe is annoyed by his brother's thoughts. I feel his body tense. "Yes, he does." Mike gives him back the same energy in his words. That's weird. Why does Genesis have to know everything? Simone clears her throat catching my attention. "Merci, will you just tell the story. Quan orders.

I take in a deep breath. "Just so we are all clear this the first and only time I will tell this story, ya'll can tell Genesis later if you feel the need to.

CHAPTER 17

Merci and Gabe

I have my Walkman on full blast for this ride to Camp Holy Mines. It's a three-hour drive to the camp hidden in the country. Yes, Unity is a small country town, However Camp Holy Mines is what I call God's Country, the nature, streams of water hidden in the woods, beautiful green grass, dirt roads, the small houses placed perfectly within the woods, the wildlife, and the breathtaking lake. I listen to my music, while enjoying the scenery outside of the car window. Plus, I do not want to hear the twins talk about what they have done and want to do to females.

Mike volunteered to drive his car last week when my dad told us we are up on the list to be counselors this summer. Last night he gave us a speech to be on our best behavior, because most of the other counselors would be from the church in Pratt, Church or not Pratt will always be our rivals.

We arrive at the camp and are given our cabin numbers, along with a list of rules, and the kids assigned to us. I see the boy counselors outnumber the girl counselors. I also peep one of the star players from Pratt is one of the counselors. I have not met him officially, however I accidentally walked up on him and our starting quarterback's girlfriend on the bus, when I had to go back because I forgot my pom-poms, I doubt he saw me. I smile and bite my bottom lip looking at his name.

"Don't even think about it." Gabe says standing over my shoulder. "Think about what?" Mike is so nosey. "Merci, here is smiling, because our enemy is here." "Who?" Mike goes on alert looking around. "Brantley's punk ass." Gabe's answer causes the lady passing out the counselor packet to look up at him, he shrugs his shoulders. "I'm going to settle in, see ya'll in a little while I say. "No, we'll walk with you." Gabe looks down at me. "Bro, you can be on Merci duty, I just saw a hunny I want." Mike is rubbing his hands together as if the chick is a meal and he is starving as he walks away. Looking up at Gabe I say, "Looks like it's just you and me." "I'm good with that." He picks up both our bags and we begin walking to the cabins.

There are a lot of kids none of us counselors have time to relax, but it feels good being here. I love the nature it's so freeing. The church in charge of this particular camp told us on Saturday upon our arrival, they will be taking over with the children Wednesday evening. Leaving us teenagers to hangout and relax. They made it clear that this camp may not be on sacred grounds, however God sees and knows all things. I laugh at them using God as a scare tactics, on horny teenagers, that will not be under adult supervision for almost three days. That part of the speech has nothing to do with me, since we've been here, I've spent time with Gabe and the children assigned to us. I know when the children are re-assigned to the adults, he will be hanging with his brother.

Wednesday around noon the kids began to pack up and move to the cabins closer to the sanctuary. Now the vibe feels like and 80's horror movie being left with a bunch of teenagers by a big lake. Pratt Baptist church has 26 teens here in the wilderness, those kids can't behave in their own town, so this should be interesting to see how they show out. I get sad thinking of Gabe. I'm going to miss his company. He's probably out on the prowl for chicks right now with Mike.

Looking out the dusty cabin window the full moon enhances the beauty of the lake. Making the decision to put on my swimsuit and go relax.

With the kids gone I have a cabin to myself, the girls from Pratt chose to move into cabins with each other, I didn't expect an invite. Cool with me. The only thing is I have don't access to a phone other than the one outside by the showers, however it not available, it is in constant use. I miss Simone, I've been sending up silent prayers everyday that Quan hasn't been doing anything to piss her off, my prayers may be in vain, but I still send the prayers.

Putting on my hot pink one piece bathing suit, adding coconut oil to make my skin I bump into that Brantley dude somewhere near the lake. He is sexy. There is a knock on the cabin door, since I'm heading out, I grab my towel and slip on my flip-flops, then head for the door, where the knocking has not come to an end. I stop in front of the mirror to give myself a check i-in complimenting myself with a wink. Opening the door, I can't hold my smile even though I'm not sure how to feel, I'm happy he is standing here in front of me.

"I figured you would be hanging with Mike tonight." Gabe is standing on the step below me, which has us face to face. "Yeah, my brother disappeared on me earlier, I don't feel like looking for him, and I was thinking maybe you could use the company." he smirks at me. "Your eyes are sexy, Gabe." I blurt out accidently, but the words are true. "Um, thank you." my out of the blue compliment threw him off. He bites his bottom lip while dropping his head Gabe looks me up and down. "Are you heading for a swim?" he asked, probably just to break the silence, I look at the white towel in my hand, do a full circle turn as if I'm in a pageant. I'm back face to face with him, "looks that way, you want to join me?" I ask him, not expecting him to say 'yes', a little over a year ago I wouldn't have had to ask him, however things have changed. The twins showed me that this past school year. "Hell yeah, let's go!" His voice if filled with excitement. Gabe grabs my arm not holding the towel. "You want to go change first?" looking at the jean shorts, white polo shirt, and the high-top Nikes. "No, I'll be fine." I want to agree with the word 'fine' that comes out of his mouth, but this time I control myself. I start thinking, what is going on with me. Why would I tell Gabe his eyes are sexy? Then I look at the big beautiful full moon, that's the reason. Full moons make people say and do things out of character, at least that's what my grandma told me.

Honestly, I've always had a crush on Gabe. He and Mike however Gabe has a light that shines from within him, he is so sweet, Mike is rough and doesn't think before he acts. My dad says that Mike will Gabe's downfall.

As we get closer to the lake Gabe intertwines his fingers with mine, making me nervous. I focus on the moon, because I refuse to let my inexperience with guys peak out now. "I like when you wear your hair down, Merci." He compliments quietly, before I can thank him, I get cut off by a voice in the shadows. "Shit, I do too." I turn to see who is talking, because I don't recognize the voice. Gabe tightens his grip on my hand as he turns in the direction the voice is coming from. "Nigga, you got to be out of your mind." Letting go of my hand and walks up to Brantley. Oh shit!

****

"Wait bitch! You didn't tell me about none of this." Simone is sitting up on Quan's lap looking at me as if I've betrayed her in some way. I roll my eyes at her. "Real talk, I can't stand that dude." Mike adds looking at Quan. "Do ya'll want me to finish the story or not?" "Yeah, it is kind of juicy." I take another deep breath, "anyway."

CHAPTER 18

Apparently, Brantley didn't feel Gabe walking up on him, or he didn't care. "I'm Brantley. What's your name beautiful?" he asks loudly over Gabe's shoulder I don't answer, no matter how much I want to, because it is the polite thing to do. Brantley's shirt is off, but Gabe is blocking my view, the moonlight is hitting, his arms are ripped with muscles. "Don't talk to her", Gabe talks to him. "Or what?" Brantley's answer is full of sarcasm.

Gabe has Brantley on the ground so fucking fast, "Or I'll kill you, I heard how you rock nigga, it's not fun when you are not in control is it?" Gabe's voice is calm, but authoritative. Brantley isn't putting up a fight. "Okay, okay. I got you." Brantley pleas he's barely able to get his hand up to give the signal that he gives up. "Gabe!" let him up I yell my voice giving into the laughter I had been holding in. Gabe looks over his shoulder giving me an evil smile. "You want me to let him up?" "Yes." I answer, trying to stop laughing. I'm not sure why I'm laughing, because laughing is not supposed to be included in situations like this. "Okay." He let's up on Brantley just a little. Brantley looks up at me, I can't deny he is handsome. "Sike!" Gabe yells, then slams the boy's head back into the gravel, that move stops my laughter, because I see blood. "Gabe! Let him go you're going to get in trouble.

"Merci, what you don't know is Brantley likes to play rough, or at least that's what I've been told." Gabe is talking to me but looking down at Brantley. "Bitch ass nigga." Gabe gives Brantley's head one last hard push into the gravel, then uses Brantley's chest as a prop to get up. Gabe is looking at me smiling wiping the invisible dust off of him, I shake my head as he walks back over to me and grabs my hand. Continuing our walk to the more private section of the lake, as if nothing happened.

"All of that over a football rivalry?" I want to know. "None of that had anything to do with football, I promise. He's just not a good person." Deciding not to question any further, I trust Gabe, and will take his word for it.

Reaching the dock, I remove my flip-flops, place my towel on top of the shoes, and go sit at the end of the dock letting my feet dangle in the warm water. God creates the most beautiful things." Gabe says sitting beside me, he's removed his shirt and shoes. It's not the moon driving me crazy it's Gabe. "Yes, God does create masterpieces" I say to break the awkward silence, I feel Gabe staring at me. "I like you, Merci." "I like you too". To break this silence and confusion I slide off the edge of the dock. Going underwater swimming a good way out from the dock. I'm confused because I have witnessed Gabe "likes' a lot of girls.

I re-surface above water, however Gabe is right behind me. I look up at the moon, it seems bigger or closer. "Merci," I cut him off. I do like Gabe, but I'm not one of those girls. "Stop it, you don't like me, you're bored out here." I look him in the eyes, "honestly, I thought we were better than that, "then Gabe cuts me off. "This is why I never stepped to you, because I knew you would be thinking about me like that. Listen, there are plenty of chicks out here I can literally be inside right now, but I'm out here with you in my boxers, in the middle of a fucking lake, shouldn't that show or mean something to you." He finishes.

This sucks because his curly hair is dripping wet and under the moonlight it just looks as if glitter is falling from his hair, his eyelashes appear as if he's been crying from the water, his big plush lips are dripping water, and I'm feeling the need to kiss him. I'm sure that the Actor Allan Payne has to be related to the twins in some kind of way. Focusing away from his look, and focusing on the words he just said, Gabe wants me to feel like it's a privilege for him being out here with me, and he can be somewhere right now literally inside another chick. "You're her because you want a challenge, those chicks you are talking about wouldn't think twice about letting you inside them, Gabe I'm telling you to literally go find one, because I'm going back to the cabin." I purposely splash water on him as I swim back to the dock.

I wrap my towel around my waist, slide my flip-flops on my feet, then turn around, Gabe is still in the same spot I left him floating in the water. The moonlight reflecting off the water gives Gabe a glowing aura. Tears are forming in my eyes. What if he does like me? Reminding myself of all the different girls he's kissed openly at school not caring who sees, the walking past me in the hallway as if we don't know each other, the times when the twins and I were inseparable, and I want to cuss him out or bang his head against some gravel. All of that, and now he likes me. Nigga please. "Gabe I would appreciate if you would treat me like you do back home." "And how is that?" he as finally getting back to the dock. "Like I don't exist."

Walking away from him is hard, and the water from the wet towel is weighing me down making the short walk back to the cabin feel as if it's going to take forever. Setting back to the cabin I freshen up and get in bed, looking around at the emptiness feeling alone. Similar to the feeling I initially felt when Gabe and Mike made it clear they had moved on but forgot to tell me.

****

"Wait, you told my best friend you could have been fucking other bitches for what? That's your idea of a compliment? Merci, keep going with this story, but that's whack Gabe." Simone gives me a look. I can't read what's she's trying to communicate with her eyes. However, her look causes me to ease up off Gabe's chest, he tries pulling me back in and I tense up letting him know to stop. "Why ya'll left her like that? I'm a real G and that makes me sad." Quan shakes his head at Gabe. "We didn't leave her as I said before, we had to fall back. "Mike answers, I didn't turn to look at his face, but in his voice, I can hear the remorse in his voice. Gabe tries again to pull me in, I don't resist. He whispers in my ear, "I'm sorry." "Merci, finish telling the story, I'm sorry we made you feel that, but look at us now."

"Yeah, look at ya'll now." My heart starts to race at the sound of his voice. The energy in the room shifts. "Happy birthday, Merci." He says, handing me a single red rose, he takes the recliner next to Mike in the back. "This shit is nice." I hear him say.

The only thing I hate about the new high-tech security system, that my dad just had to have is if the power goes out instead of everything going on lock, it unlocks everything. Giving free access to the house. I wonder how long and how much of the story has he heard, because we've been all ben so engrossed in the story, that he could have come in at any time and none of us would have known. "I like the story. Are you going to finish telling it Merci?" well that answers the question I had of how long he has been listening. Obviously, the whole time, and he's just deciding to join us in the room. That's weird. I make no eye contact. "Yeah." Is my response, although I'm waiting for my heart rate to regulate. The words are at the tip of the tongue, when Simone asks, "Genesis, where did you find a rose with no thrones?"

****

CHAPTER 19

After letting a few tears fall, about what happened at the lake. I prayed to God for peace, then fell asleep fast. The next morning Mike walks in the cabin without knocking, but I am awake, or my eyes had adjusted to the bright sunlight shining through. He still should have knocked. I could have been naked in here. "You excited for tonight?" he asks sitting on one of the empty beds. "What is tonight, oh shit the party we aren't supposed to have, but we do anyway? No." my answer is dry. "You, okay?" I nod my head 'yes' to his question. He and I both know that I am lying.

"Honestly Mike I'm ready to go home, I can care less about a party." He stands up, comes over to where I'm standing and gives me a big hug not knowing how bad I needed that hug. Mike heads for the door, "Well, I'm about to go do what I do best." We both laugh. "Let me guess, go be a dog?" "Yes, ma'am you are correct, and today my brother has finally decided to join me." He says, then heads out the cabin quickly. I feel my anger surfacing, but I remind myself, tomorrow this will all be over.

Mike wasn't lying about him and his brother being dogs today. They are even starting early. As I walk out of the cabin, heading towards the snack machines. There the twins are each standing with a girl under their arm. Gabe makes eye contact with me long enough to keep my attention to watch him give the girl with him a kiss on the cheek. I smile and give him a wink, because at some point today or tonight, I'm going to find that Brantley dude and see how Gabe reacts when he gets a taste of his own medicine.

****

"Hold up!" Simone yells trying to jump out of Quan's lap. "Baby what's wrong?" Simone's out burst has us all caught off guard. "Nope, nope, and nope! Gabe you like to play games I got you though. Merci, finish this story up Simone demands. "Hmph." Comes from Genesis. I ease off Gabe's chest again, this time he doesn't try to pull me back in. That's weird. I continue with the story.

****

I spend the rest of my day going to the lake, take a swim, take a walk soaking in the sunshine and nature, then enjoy the rest of the day by reading to relax my mind. Basically, waiting for the night to begin. I figure if I can't find Brantley, I'm sure there's another guy I can use to get Gabe in his feelings. I truly thought there was a difference between him and mike, but obviously I was wrong.

My dad did a Bible study once on angels, he mentioned that 'Gabriel' is Go's trusted messenger angel. On the flip side he added this same angel's intentions are questionable, what a as I think about that now.

I start to hear the other counselors outside, the music is getting louder, and that signals the festivities are in full swing. I have my dark blue daisy duke's cutoff shorts, tight ribbed hot pink tank top, and matching hot pink flip-flops. My hair is up in a messy bun, being in this true nature environment has me feeling myself. I look over at the mirror, before I walk out giving myself a thumbs up. I am fine ass hell.

Heading to the coolers to get a soda, I use the moment to over sexualize myself with the way I bend over to get a drink out of the cooler. "Damn ma!" I roll my eyes grabbing a drink, because I know when I turn around Mike will be standing there. Not only is Mike standing here with some random chick, but Gabe is also with him, however he is solo, for now at least. "Your dad would kill you if he was here and saw you in those shorts." Mike statement is true, but it doesn't stop him from looking and licking his lips. "You look hot girl. The random dark skin chick wearing all black compliments me, I give her a genuine smile, "Thank you."

"Merci, I left something in your cabin last night." Gabe barely gets the words out, before he snatches my hand walking me to the cabin. "You didn't come in my cabin last night." "Shut up!" is all he says. That's rude. We get in the cabin Gabe locks the door behind us. "So, you want them dudes to see how your pussy sits up in those short, you want them dudes looking at them titties, or you want them rubbing all over your ass?" I shrug both shoulders at the questions he has asked me. He walks up to me, and I look up at him. "Do you want me to?" I answer him by taking off my shirt, then sit on the bed. He approaches slowly kissing on my neck while unbuttoning my shorts, sliding his hand inside. I'm not wearing any panties, so he has easy access.

I moan loudly, because whatever he is doing is driving me crazy. "I want you to be loud," he says. "I want to know how to please you." Gabe pushes me all the way back on the bed, pulling off his t-shirt, leaving his purple gym shorts on. He climbs closer on top of me on the bed, I lift up to my lips with hi, however no kiss. Using his left hand and unhooks my bra sliding it off I throw it on the floor, he moves further down pulling my shorts off.

Gabe's tongue works my body, by the time he gets to work between my legs the fireworks outside have begun to sound off. I scream freely, Gabe is between my legs moaning and slurping, his fingers pinching and twisting my nipples. I feel a sensation causing my legs to shake, my clit is throbbing, and Gabe keeps saying, "Give it to me Merci." And "Just let it go."

A knock comes on the door I shoot up, but Gabe eases me back down. The knocking doesn't stop, I tune it out, because the sensation comes back, "Give it to me baby." I release and Gabe goes crazy, grabbing my hips, pulling me in closer to him, and he drinks from my body. I don't know what Gabe has just done to me, nut in this moment he has my head gone. Feels as if he sucked my soul out of my bod.

Gabe stands up my wetness covering his face and chest, knowing that he is all soaked because of me makes him look sexier. "That's my pussy you understand me?" he states. The knocking begins again, before I can say at "Okay" to Gabe claiming ownership over my pussy. I put my clothes on quickly then jump on a random bunk pretending to read a magazine. Gabe pulls his shirt on quietly unlocks the door. "Come in." he yells. He pretends as if he's getting back to doing push ups on the floor, that will throw Mike off if he asks why his brother is wet. Mike walks in looks at me then his brother, "Ya'll boring", he says as if he's annoyed and leaves.

****

"Merci, get up, because I'm about to knock this nigga out for playing with you like that." Simone gets off Quan's lap, he doesn't restrain her. Fuck, I knew this story should have stayed between Gabe and I.

CHAPTER 20

"That's whack!" Simone says anger in her voice. "What?" I question. "He played you," her gaze burning through Gabe. "I bet he is playing you or trying to play you now." She is serious. I stand up slowly by Simone in front of Gabe.

"The story is a good story but let me add before I go in on Gabe. I know Quan and I have our problems. However, he doesn't play the jealousy game with me." She's speaking the truth Quan has never flaunted a chick in front of her when they break up for a day or so. "Gabe has been playing head games with you before that church camp stuff. I get the whole protection stuff too, but that's what friends do, protect each other, most dudes are in a relationship with the chick they are protecting." Simone is still speaking nothing but the truth. "Guess what Gabe, I'm Merci's protector as well, hearing that story, then you still flaunt bitches in her face, that's weird. I was on your side, but Merci don't choose him."

"Quan, get your girl. "Gabe sounds off. "Nope, my baby has a point." Quan will not go against Simone. Gabe turns to look at Mike for back up, but only receives a shoulder shrug from his twin. "Gabe only wants you when someone else does, probably why he's tripping about Genesis so bad." Simone finishes by pointing out the obvious.

As if on cue the electricity shoots back on, Gabe reaches for me, I slap his hand away. Simone is right. My anger is peaking, I give Simone a twisted smile signaling to her that I am about to explode. "All right guys it's time for us to go and I don't know a lot about God, however lights coming back on while it's still storming is a clear sign for us to bounce." Gabe is up and out the front door. Simone gives me a big hug. I let her know we will talk later.

Not paying attention I turn around, bumping face first into Genesis' chest. I breath his scent in, before I look up at him. He's not smiling, he's just standing with a grim look on his face. "I guess it's just you and me now." The assurance in his voice lets me believe I'm going to let him stay. Does he have amnesia about yesterday and the day before that? He's just like Gabe. That's weird. He is wrong, it's beginning to settle in my spirit that when it comes to Genesis and his crew, they all love to play games.

"You guessed wrong. I want you to leave." I'm telling him to leave, however I want him to stay. "Simone is right I enjoy spending my birthdays alone." "I can respect that." Walking around me to get to the front door, looking up and around the house. "You do know one day I'm going to buy us a house like this one day." Opening the door and closing it behind him.

Am I the one going crazy? Was yesterday evening, with Genesis and Gabe a dream? I remember the rose Genesis presented to me for my birthday, and a pass for him letting himself in the house. Maybe, he wanted to listen, until he knew it would be best for him to make his presence felt. I go back to the entertainment room to retrieve the rose. I left it on the arm of the chair I had been sitting on Gabe's lap in, I cringe thinking of Gabe. Making a mental note to thank Simone tor her honesty pertaining to the story, she's always been good at reading into situations, except when it comes to Quan.

Heading upstairs, I remove my hoodie and sweatpants that I had thrown on earlier. I hop back into bed, beginning to think what and how my mom would have planned my 16th birthday if she were alive.

Not sure, but at some point, while I had been daydreaming about my mom, I fell asleep. The rain is pounding hard on the roof, the thunder is rolling loud across the sky. I peep over at my alarm it's 8pm on the dot. I needed the sleep, from Tuesday up until this morning my body inside and out has been through a lot.

Getting up to prepare myself for my birthday celebration even though I'm celebrating alone. Loving my new black lace dress, I feel as if I look and feel more mature for the first time today, than I did yesterday. Peeping through the blinds of my window, and the rain is not letting up. The lighting coming from the waterfall is beautiful. "Sorry mama." I whisper, as if she can hear me. The phone rings, "Hello." my voice is wavering. "What's wrong Babygirl?" my dad asks. "It's raining." No longer able to hold my tears back. "I'm sorry, Merci, I promise we will celebrate when I get home. Please stop crying, however I am sure the Lord has good reasoning for the weather." his voice is calming and convincing. "Also, I'm sorry I forgot to order your cupcakes." Cupcakes are the last thing on my mind, "It's okay daddy, I miss you so much," I tell him, it's starting to set in that I am alone. I let the tears fall freely, not wiping them away.

"Babygirl, order a pizza and I will call Gabriel to go pick it up for you." "No!" I yell in the phone at the mention of Gabe's name. Waiting for my dad to scold me for raising my voice at him, I could have added 'sir' to the 'no'. "Okay Merci." his voice is cold. "I'm sorry daddy." "I forgive you, but don't raise your voice towards me again." "Yes Sir." "Now that's better, Babygirl I need to go tend to some business, try to enjoy the rest of your birthday as best as you can. I love you." he hangs up again before I'm able to say, "I love you too."

CHAPTER 21

I feel disappointment inside, the rain is showing no sign of letting up. I'm alone on my 16th birthday. I always believed I would be riding around town in my new car with Simone in the passenger seat. "God please let something amazing happen." I pray looking up at the ceiling of my room. Laying in my bed feeling sorry for myself isn't going to fix anything, so I decide to go downstairs. Pop some popcorn and watch a movie. I refuse to change out of my birthday dress, it deserves to be worn even if no one is here to see me in it.

Grabbing the single red rose off of my dresser, I giggle reflecting on Simone's question to Genesis, but seriously where did he find a rose without thorns? I give him credit, at least he came bearing a gift. Gabe came as himself, delivering the gift of deception. I dodged a bullet with Gabe for sure. Heading out of my bedroom, the phone rings, I hurry to the phone to answer it, because by a miracle it might be my grandma. I strongly believe in miracles.

"Bitch!" I roll my eyes hearing Simone's voice, I can barely hear her, because of all the background noise, music and a bunch of teenagers. "Simone, I can barely hear you, call me tomorrow, I'm heading downstairs to watch a movie." "Girl shut up and listen Gabe is in here tonguing Kyomi down, and Genesis is." I hang up the phone. Why would Simone call me to tell me information that could hurt my feelings?

Thinking positive in less than two years, I'll be walking across that stage, graduating, heading to college, and I'm sure that's where I will meet my husband. Those positive thoughts instantly help me feel better.

Walking downstairs I focus on not falling from the lack of lighting. Midway down the doorbell rings. "I'm coming!" I yell, because whoever it is keeps pushing the button. Opening the front door hoping it's not Sister Hazel, I freeze. "Merci, can I come in, we need to talk?" Genesis asks, breathing hard. He doesn't wait for my answer he walks pass me. "Um, you, okay?" I ask because he's soaking wet. "No, I mean yeah, I want you to choose me." He steps closer to me, I step back, and he steps closer. "Genesis what are you talking about?" My real question is why he is soaking wet, because if he drove here, he may have gotten a few raindrops on him walking from the driveway to the front door. I hit the light switch for the front porch lights to come on, then step out on the porch, and there is no car in the driveway. I step back in the house and look at him. "Dude, how did you get here?" "I walked and jumped the fence. I forgot the code to your gate."

As much as I want to run and jump up in his arms and head up to my bedroom. I know what's going to happen afterwards, he will go back to his girlfriend. I have already been his fool once. "Genesis, leave and go back to Tynesha like you did the last time." The front door is still open, I step to the side so he can exit.

He doesn't move, "Quan fucked this up, Simone did what I asked, but Quan messed up everything up!" he let's the words burst out. "Excuse me?" I push my hair behind my left ear, cocking my head to the side to make sure I'm hearing him clearly.

"You're Merci Simms, right?" he asks, I nod. Then he takes off, "The Merci Simms that sits in the balcony at her Pop's church, the Merci Simms that leaves after praise and worship service, the Merci Simms who goes to her locker number 418 after 2nd period to guzzle a soda, the Merci Simms who' Adidas gear is always fly, and the Merci Simms that takes my breath away everyday when I pretend to come in the cafeteria for an extra cup. The tears are falling from my eyes, I have no reply to his words just tears.

Genesis steps closer and lifts my chin to look up into his dark eyes, but I can see the light brown speckles within the darkness. "The Merci Simms that I walked over here in the rain and jumped a high ass fence just to ask for you to choose me.

In this moment I understand when my dad uses the phrase "you can hear the silence". "Genesis, I'm sorry, but I will not play second no matter how much I might want the person." I'm trying to keep my cool. But how can I when the guy of my dreams. The guy who I believed didn't know that existed until this past Tuesday, but he knew I existed, and he studied me. "I want you to leave, but I want to know what Simone and Wuan have to do with all of this".

"When summer camp ended for football and cheer. I peeped you during the flag football game, you were killing it, I knew I seen you before, but I couldn't place where. I pointed you out to Quan, he told me you are the pastor's daughter and Simone's best friend. Tynesha saw me checking you out and wouldn't talk to me for a week." I hold my hand up to process the information. "So, Tuesday you knew exactly who I was on the porch?" "Yes, I asked Simone to bring you. Tynesha and Kyomi weren't supposed to be there, but Quan messed that up by thinking with his dick." Genesis is breathing slower now, I guess he's been wanting to get this off his chest and didn't know how. Wait, that's why Simone asked the sisters why they were there and told them they weren't supposed to be there. Makes sense now. "I wanted to vibe with you and I'm not the cheating type, but something about you Merci."

Taking in a deep breath I turn to close the front door. I reach over to the right, almost knocking the vase of black roses over to hit the light switch. We both squint as the light illuminates the house. With clear vision he smiles at me, but I scrunch up my face to hide my smile. Looking down at where he is standing, the floor is drenched. I'll get him a towel after we finish this conversation.

Sitting Indian style on the floor not caring how unladylike with a dress on, I can't focus on how I'm sitting. I need to keep focusing on what Genesis is saying, it could be life changing, but I won't get my hopes up. "Go, on." Waving my hand for him to continue talking. "Kyomi told Tynesha about her and Quan that day, he must have gotten caught up in the moment and told her we would all be hanging at my house, because I told Tynesha we were going to shoot hoops. When they showed up, I knew that Quan had done something stupid." I shake my head Quan will never change, I feel sorry for Genesis, but what's done in the dark comes to the light. "Tynesha doesn't like me, because you were watching me play flag football?" I ask not expecting an answer, I look up at the high-rise ceiling. That's weird. "Pretty much she's extremely possessive and jealous, but I don't sweat her about the guys she sneaks around with." "Hold up, you know that she cheats?" he puts his head down. "Yeah, but she had a screwed-up childhood, I can't fault her actions, inside she is a beautiful person, but I can't help. I have mad love for her, I'm just not in love with her." He looks down at me on the floor. I get it, Genesis is a good person, and how can I be mad at that.

"I called Mike the day after the flag football game thinking he might have the scoop on you, he lied telling me ya'll don't talk or know each other like that." Hearing Genesis say that Mike lied to him about knowing me stings my heart.

Genesis is standing there as if he's waiting for me to say something. I have nothing left to say now, and I feel bad, because he has to be freezing in those wet clothes. I stand reaching over, making sure not to knock the roses over, to flip the light switch off. I walk pass him heading up the stairs. Midway, I turn around looking down at him, I can see the light brown speckles mixing with the darkness in his eyes reflecting from the random night lights placed throughout the house. I shrug my shoulders and ask, "are you coming?".

CHAPTER 22

I wait on the stairs for him to catch up with me, he grabs my hand, but I take lead, by pulling his hand to follow me to my room. Letting go of his hand when we get to the door, I don't turn around to ask, "Are you and her completely over?" "Completely, I swear.", his answer comes out quick. Genesis grabs me around the waist spinning me around, closing my eyes knowing his next move. His lips feel like marshmallows on mine, our tongues begin to play with each other. I hear us both moaning I try pushing him away not realizing he has me off the floor and up against my bedroom door. "Dude, you have to get of these wet clothes." He smiles at me His hand that is holding my ass up moves forward to where my wetness is between my legs. Genesis bites his bottom lip, breathing hard as he rubs my clit through my panties. "Choose me?"

"What?" I ask while trying to catch my breath. "Merci, I'm not going in that room until you choose me." He has me at eye level now, he's good at what he's doing, he slides my panties to the side. I'm glad my pussy is shaved to perfection. His touch is right on point. "Say it!"

he demands, adding pressure to the slow circular motion against my clit. My legs begin to quiver. "I choose you. It's always been you." I can barely get the words out. We start kissing again, as he slowly lowers me back on the floor. With both of my feet back on the ground, he steps back. I break eye contact, looking down and bust out laughing, surprisingly Genesis joins is. I look at his eyes as he's laughing and I fall deeper in love, his eyes hold so much love, that means his eyes hold a lot of other things inside as well. I'll figure out exactly what they hold as time goes.

This has been a crazy week." I get out between giggles. "You and me both." He reaches across me to open my bedroom door. "Why is everything out there light, but your joint is dark, like literally?" Genesis asks. I can't see him, as I'm navigating my way through the dark to get to my lamp on my nightstand. This guy moves like a vampire, he's standing behind me with his shirt off, by the time I turn the light on. His sudden closeness causes me to stumble back, he catches me with his right hand.

Once we are both on the bed, I know this is the night Genesis is going to make me a woman, in a good way. With that thought, I feel Genesis should meet at least one of my parents, even if it will be awkward.

"Wait, wait," as much as don't want to I push Genesis' chest up, he gives a deep sigh. "I need you to meet my mom." I request, knowing he might think I'm insane. "Cool" is his answer. Wow, he's okay with this. "Put your shirt on," he's questioning nothing. Feeling bad watching him search for that wet wife beater. "Dude." I point to my bathrobe hanging from my bathroom door. He gives me a fake grin. However, I choose to focus on his muscular chest.

"Merci, I'm cool with this, but please don't tell me your mom is somewhere in here." I watch him start to look around as if we have been watched this whole time. I smile, "No, she's outside." I'm standing by the window, I've had the shades open all day, but before I pull up the blinds. I pull my dress back up. "I'll have it all the way off in a minute." He whispers rubbing the small of my back. I giggle looking over at him in my cute bathrobe that I know if he moves the wrong way will rip apart.

Pulling the string to lift the blinds, the rain is at a light drizzle, unlocking the handles I lift the window. "Holy shit! Ya'll backyard is the spot." Genesis' head is out the window trying to see everything. He is right my dad made sure that our backyard is both private and sacred. The big, beautiful color changing waterfall, the marble bench made to sit and admire the place his wife resides. The landscaping is beautiful, the trees planted along the back fence, not giving a place to try and peak through, and the grass makes me imagine the Garden of Eden, just we have the bootleg version.

I nudge Genesis and look down and smile at the waterfall. "Mama, this Genesis. Genesis this is my Mama her name is Glory." My eyes stay on the waterfall, the lights are transitioning to emerald green as if she is present. He inches closer to me, placing his hand on mine. "Nice to meet you Mrs. Glory." Confusion in his voice, and I understand that. "My dad had her ashes mixed in with the cement bricks." I explain intertwining my fingers with his.

Mrs. Glory, Merci is amazing I only have good intentions towards her." His voice is sincere. "So, you really are single?" I ask smiling. "No, I have a girlfriend. I thought you knew that before we came in the room." He's still looking at the waterfall in a trance. Snatching my hand away from his. "Bye mama!" I yell. Pulling the window down, not caring if his head gets caught in the middle.

"Get out!" I yell, pointing to my room door. "I was about to give you, my virginity. Didn't you tell me you and Tynesha are completely over, but now you have a girlfriend, but now you have a girlfriend you lied Genesis." I can't control the yelling, but I can control my temper. Focusing on the red numbers on my alarm clock, it's 11:11pm, making a silent wish to not cry in front of him right now.

"Why are you bugging, I'm with my girlfriend, you're my girlfriend right? You said before we came in this room that you choose me." His thick eyebrows are raised, and the darkness is all I see in his eyes. "Oh, I'm your girlfriend." I cover my mouth feeling stupid.

Animalistic is how Genesis is staring at me. "Merci, take everything off, get on the bed and lay on your back." His voice is low and sexy. I follow his directions. I feel his weight as he gets on the bed. Coming into view and closer to me all I can think is he is perfect. I know that this is right. Fuck! Simone's voice pop in my head, "girl I'm not going to lie, the first-time hurts." My body tenses, "Relax bae." Genesis says, feeling his soft lips kissing my thighs, only kissing my clit once, then blowing on it as if it needs to cool down. He moves up giving each of my nipples a kiss. He is on top of me, laying on my back, his body looks massive from my viewpoint. "You trust me?" he asks looking down at me. I nod nod yes. I can feel him trembling, realizing he's nervous as well. Genesis spreads my legs with him knees, holding himself up in the pushup position.

Taking his right arm causing his weight to shift to his left side. "Damn, you are wet." He says with a moan, I feel his fingers massaging my clit and exploring where the wetness is coming from. "Ouch." I whisper when he attempts sliding his finger inside of me. "You sure you cool with this?" he asks bringing his hand back up. I nod yes again. "Say it." He demands. "I want this, I promise." My words are met with a deep hard kiss, Genesis allows his body weight to fall on me. While we are kissing, he grabs an extra pillow on the bed, "lift your hips," he instructs quickly, I do as he asks. Dude is heavy on top of me, feeling the tip of his dick ready to enter inside of me. Giving me another deep kiss, I feel an unfamiliar sting. The kiss is meant to distract me. "You, okay?" he lifts up, but keeps stroking slowly inside of me, the pressure only lasts a little bit, but this feels amazing. He continues, no words are being said just moaning coming from both of us. It's as if we are trying to blend our bodies together, my legs are strapped tight around his body, and he is stroking as slow and deep as he can. His dick starts to swell causing my pussy to explode on it and he begins to stroke faster, gripping my hips tighter and pulling me down, holding me down as he explodes inside of me.

He is kissing me repeating, "Damn" in between the kisses. Finally, removing himself from on top of me, Genesis pulls into his arms, I didn't realize how big he is I feel so small against him. "How was that, was I too rough? Will you want to do it again? Be honest Merci how did it feel?" I think the questions are cute. Nuzzling closer to him, "all I know is you feel like home Genesis."

CHAPTER 23

After spending all weekend together, to now getting out of Genesis' car on this beautiful Monday morning. I'll be walking in with him as his girlfriend, it seems unreal, but it is real. I love him, I'm in love with him, and I don't care who likes it or not. Especially since I spoke with my dad about it on the phone last night. I told him everything that had taken place. Gabe is definitely on his shit list, as well as mine.

My dad wanted to talk to speak with Genesis immediately on the phone. I went upstairs while they spoke. After their conversation, Genesis joined me about an hour later. He looked shook, "you okay?" I asked. "Yeah, your Pops is different from what I thought. "Does he want you to stay away from me?" "No, he did tell me God is merciful, but if I break your heart, he will show me no mercy." I laughed, but Genesis didn't join in.

"You ready?" he asks putting his arm around me. "Yes, it's different, well for me it is, you've done this before, but with someone else." High-key I'm nervous. "No, Merci this completely different for me too." He says I look up at him, smiling at the light brown speckles that are dancing in the darkness in his eyes. "Let go bae, I love you." Those last three words came out fast, I don't think he meant for those words to slip out.

To make things awkward for him on purpose, I start walking not waiting for Genesis. "Merci." I'm smiling, imagining his facial expression, his thick eyebrows scrunching together. My smile grows wider, because I can feel his gaze piercing through the back of my head. Collecting myself, I look over my shoulder. "Dude, I love you too." Rolling my eyes, as he catches up to me. "That's what I thought." Kissing me on the forehead. Genesis opens the door leading to the main hallway. Here we go.

"Bitch you are glowing and stuff, dick must be amazing." Simone says rushing to me before I get to my locker. Genesis starts laughing. "Catch you at lunch bae, and don't tell this loudmouth girl our business." He says playfully pointing at Simone, she slaps his hand away. Giving me one more kiss on the forehead, then he walks off with Quan. I feel weird watching him walking away until he looks back at me and mouths, "I love you." All I can do is smile. "Nigga you in love already?" Quan is loud causing most of the people in the hallway to look my way.

"Girl, everyone knows you and Genesis are together." "I wonder how they know that?" I roll my eyes at Simone as I get my locker open. Merci, look." She says nudging me.

Gabe and Mike come in the main hallway doors with two familiar chicks. Gabe is holding hands with Kyomi and Mike has his arm around Tynesha. Both sisters shoot us mean mugs as they walk pass by as if their new pairing is supposed to mean something. Simone and I look at each other, "that's weird". We say in unison, and head to our first period classes.

The school week flies by and it has been fun. Genesis and I are a good fit. My dad is anxious to get home, he wants Genesis to come over for dinner Saturday. My Grandma Eve is skeptical but can't wait to meet my first boyfriend. I told Genesis I better not catch him flirting with my grandma, because she is beautiful.

Today is Friday, Genesis says he needs to play his best tonight for the team to make it to the play-offs, whatever that is. Genesis, Quan, Gabe, and Mike are going to pull through with the win. I told Genesis last night that I want to walk to school, he tried to argue with me about it, but I won.

Reaching the bottom of the hill, leading to the crossing, I see the cop cars, like a lot of cop cars in the school parking lot.

"Get off of them!" dropping my bookbag, running as fast I can to get to Simone, because I know her that's her voice screaming. I see a cop pushing her back. I get to her, catching her gaze leads me to see the 4 dudes on the ground laying facedown, handcuffed. Quan, Gabe, Mike, and Genesis. Looking up to see the dogs are barking at. Cops are pulling black duffle bags out of the trunks of the boys' cars.

These are not our small town cops, I don't see the Chief anywhere. Wait! This means Genesis lied to me. "How did you and your crew get those nice cars, I asked looking at him, he was occupied reading through my journals looking for his name. "A college gave them to us, a recruitment bribe, we aren't supposed to accept gifts, but who is going to pass up on a new whip." His answer came out so easy. I had no reason not to believe him or keep asking questions.

"Genesis, no." comes out as a whisper, tears take over my eyes, causing my vision to blur, and all the loud talking and barking from the dogs, sound as is I'm underwater. I catch a glimpse of Tynesha and Kyomi over in the cut crying, and I honestly feel sorry for Tynesha. Turning my back as the police begin to get the boys up to walk and place them to the police cars. When I turn back around, they are all gone, including their cars. I go sit by Simone who is now on her knees crying.

I race home, there is no way I can be at school after what just took place. Reaching the top of the hill, I see my dad's car in the driveway. He must have just gotten home, because the front door is open. "Daddy!" I yell. Glad he is standing right inside the doorway, as if he's been waiting for me. "Babygirl, everything is going to be alright." He consoles me with his voice and this hug. "You know?" "Yeah, the twins' mother just left, I assured her that I will do what I can to help those boys." Pulling back looking up at my favorite person. Asking him a question with my eyes, waiting for his answer. "Yes, Merci even your boy." I jump back in his arms. "Thank you, daddy I'm glad you're home." "Me too, Babygirl, but remember worrying is a sin and all that ugly crying you are doing is going to cause you premature wrinkles. Go upstairs and get some rest. "I love you." My dad says releasing me from his tight hug. I head for the stairs, "I love you too, Daddy."

Two months after the arrest all four boys took the plea deal for a year and a day in prison. Quan made phone calls to Simone everyday for those two months, when they were in county. He also allowed her to come visit.

Genesis didn't call me at all and declined my visits. "You sure you want to do this?" Simone quietly asks me. "I feel it's best." We have driven my all new '94 Honda Accord, for 5 hours to get to this place. It would make no sense for me to back out now. "I'm going to stay out here." Simone lets me know as we pull in the parking lot. "I'll let them know my driver is waiting our here." I grab her hand, because I understand this is something I have to do alone. We both have tears in our eyes. "I love you." "I love you too chick." I reply meaning it. Walking up to what looks as if to have once been a building used for something great back in the day. I walk the building silently asking God to forgive me repeatedly, until I reach the front desk. "How can I help you?" the receptionist asks looking up at me annoyed.

I take a deep breath, trying not to burst out crying with my words. "Yes, my name is Merci Simms, I have an appointment for an abortion.

BOOK 2 COMING ASAP

ABOUT THE AUTHOR

Just a small town girl

Livin' in a lonely world

She took the midnight train goin' anywhere

Just a city boy

Born and raised in south Detroit

He took the midnight train goin' anywhere

~Journey

CPSIA information can be obtained
at www.ICGtesting.com
Printed in the USA
LVHW081513090622
720760LV00017B/1613